CAMILLA LACKBERG

SWEET REVENGE

TWO NOVELLAS

Translated from the Swedish by Ian Giles

HarperCollins*Publishers*

HarperCollins*Publishers* Ltd
1 London Bridge Street,
London SE1 9GF

www.harpercollins.co.uk

HarperCollins*Publishers*
1st Floor, Watermarque Building, Ringsend Road
Dublin 4, Ireland

This paperback edition 2022
1

A catalogue record for this book is available from the British Library

ISBN: 978-0-00-835446-6 (PB b-format)
ISBN: 978-0-00-835447-3 (PB a-format)

Set in Sabon Lt Std by Palimpsest Book Production Ltd, Falkirk, Stirlingshire

Printed and Bound in the UK using 100% Renewable Electricity at
CPI Group (UK) Ltd

MIX
Paper from
responsible sources
FSC™ C007454

This book is produced from independently certified FSC™ paper
to ensure responsible forest management.

For more information visit: www.harpercollins.co.uk/green

For Meja and Polly

WOMEN WITHOUT MERCY

PART 1

1. Ingrid Steen

When her husband Tommy came into the living room, Ingrid Steen cupped her hand around the object she was holding, placing it in the crack between the sofa cushions.

He walked past her.

He flashed her a quick, mechanical smile before continuing into the kitchen. She could hear him as he opened the fridge and rifled inside it, humming Bruce Springsteen's 'The River' to himself.

Ingrid left the object where it was and got up from the sofa. She drifted over to the window. The street lighting was struggling against the Scandinavian darkness. The bushes and trees were bare and contorted. There was a TV flickering in the house opposite.

Behind her, Tommy cleared his throat and Ingrid spun around.

'How was your day?'

She contemplated him without answering. He was holding a half-eaten, cold meatball in one hand. In the other he had a glass of milk. His hair was thinning on the top – it always had been, but in his thirties he'd had the good taste to shave his head. The bottom of his shirt was wrinkled after being tucked into his trousers all day.

'Good.'

Tommy smiled.

'Great.'

She watched as he left. *Tommy*. A working-class name. *Bruce Springsteen*. A working-class hero. Nevertheless, as soon as he'd been made editor-in-chief of Sweden's biggest tabloid, *Aftonpressen*, they'd moved out to Bromma – a neighbourhood for the upper middle classes in general, and the Swedish media elite in particular.

The sound of fingers pattering away on a keyboard resumed in the study. Ingrid returned to the sofa, groping about between the cushions. She found one of her daughter Lovisa's old toys. She pulled it out, taking in the little green dinosaur with its oversized, staring eyes before placing it on the coffee table. She bent over the sofa again, found the small device and took it with her into the hallway.

The sound of fingers writing, issuing orders, amending head-lines increased in intensity. She took Tommy's coat off the hanger. The rectangular sewing kit in her back jeans pocket pressed into her buttock. Upstairs, she opened the door to the bathroom. After placing the sewing kit on the side of the basin, she locked the door and shut the toilet lid. She quickly picked open part of the inner lining of the coat, inserted the small device and checked that it worked. Using her index finger, she switched it on, and then sewed the shiny fabric together again with a couple of stitches.

2. Victoria Brunberg

Three years ago, Victoria's last name had been Volkova, she had lived in the modern Russian city of Ekaterinburg and she had vaguely remembered something about the country of Sweden from her history classes. Now her name was Victoria Brunberg, and she lived in the village of Sillbo a few miles outside of Heby, somewhere in the middle of the country. She spoke Swedish with a thick accent, and had no job or friends. She sighed as she poured the steaming hot tea into a mug emblazoned with the words *Sweden Rock*.

She could hear the wind through the cracks at the bottom of the window. Outside the window there were fields, forests and grey sky. She shaped her hand into a screen so that she wouldn't have to look at that when she took the tea over to the kitchen table. Victoria sighed and put her feet up on the table. Everything about this place – this country – was detestable. She cupped the mug of tea in her hands and closed her eyes.

'Yuri,' she whispered.

The gangster princess, that was what her friends in Ekaterinburg had jokingly called her. She had liked it. She had loved the diamonds, the drugs, the dinners, the clothes and the apartment they had lived in.

On the day of her twentieth birthday, it had all disappeared. Yuri had been murdered. By now, his body had probably decayed beyond recognition. The hairy back, the big hands, the heavy cheeks – they were all gone.

Bang, bang, bang.

Yuri had been gunned down on her birthday. The blood had spattered onto her white fur coat, which had been lying on the nightclub sofa. They had wanted to kill her too, but the murderer's third shot had missed and then he had been shot dead by Yuri's bodyguards.

She had fled to her mother's, about an hour's drive outside of town.

It had been her mother who had told her about the site where Swedish men went looking for Russian women.

'Swedish men are kind and also soft,' she'd said.

Victoria did as she was told by her mother, just as she always had done. She posted a couple of photos, received hundreds of replies in the space of a few days and picked Malte. He'd looked good in his photos – like a big baby with kind eyes. He was her age, overweight, seemed shy. He'd sent her money to buy the plane ticket and two weeks later she'd stepped across the threshold of the yellow house in Sillbo for the first time.

Outside in the courtyard, she could hear the sound of Malte's motorbike. Victoria took her feet off the table and looked out through the window. His body made the motorcycle seem small, like Godzilla on a pony. Coming along the road behind Malte was a white van. It swung in through the gate and pulled up beside the motorbike. The driver, Malte's friend Lars, opened the passenger-side door, heaved out a crate of beer and lugged it towards the front door. Malte grabbed a can, popped it open and drank from it greedily. The layers of fat on his neck undulated. Both men disappeared out of Victoria's sight and a second later she heard the key slide into the lock and turn.

They clomped in wearing their shoes. Lars hesitated when he saw the dark, mucky footprints being left by the mud on the parquet.

'Fuck it. The bitch'll be glad to have something to do. She just spends her days sitting at home,' Malte said, without looking at her.

Lars smiled sheepishly, meeting her gaze for half a second. He mumbled hello and set the crate of beer down on the table. Malte went over to the cooker.

'Let's see what sludge you've cooked up today,' he said, raising the lid. The steam made him recoil and blink his eyes. He fanned with his hand a few times and squinted into the pot. Standing beside Victoria, Lars cracked open a beer.

'Potatoes. Good. Very good.' Malte looked around the kitchen and spread out his hands.

'Is that it?'

'I didn't know when you were coming. I'll fry the sausages now,' Victoria said. Malte tittered, looking past her at his friend. He repeated her words in an exaggerated falsetto with a Russian accent. Lars snorted, beer running down his chin. 'She's a looker, but fuck me, she's not the sharpest tool in the box,' Malte said. More beer ran down Lars's chin.

Her clothes smelled of cooking. Malte had promised to fix the extractor, but he hadn't got round to it. She put the dirty plates in the dishwasher. The men were ensconced on the sofa. The coffee table was littered with empty beer cans. Before long, they would fall asleep, which was when her day began. Properly. She glanced at the sofa to see where Malte's mobile was. She was reassured when she spotted it between two beer cans.

'Should have got myself a Thai like you did. Better food. Better head,' Malte said with a burp.

'Well, send her back then?' suggested Lars with a guffaw.

'Why not? Wonder what the return policy is on mail-order bitches,' Malte said between gasps of laughter.

'No refunds. Maybe a credit note?' Lars managed to cough out.

'Yes, the product's been used. Second hand.'

Another explosion of laughter at the same moment as the water began to flow inside the dishwasher.

3. Ingrid Steen

Ingrid parked up outside Höglandsskolan Primary School, switched off the engine and sat there with her hands on the wheel. She was an hour early.

Fourteen years as a journalist, including two as an American correspondent, and more prizes than she could count. Before, the newspaper cuttings, certificates and some of the photos had been on the walls of their home. When Tommy had been made editor-in-chief, the couple had mutually agreed that it would be for the best if Ingrid stayed at home with their daughter. Being editor-in-chief for *Aftonpressen* was more than a job, it was a lifestyle. Well, that was how Tommy put it. He assured her that had it been the other way round – her being asked – then he would have made the same sacrifice.

Ingrid had made do. She had packed her career highlights into an IKEA cardboard box and put it in the furthermost corner of the attic, assuming the role of a supportive wife. Lately, her thoughts kept returning to those years she'd spent as a journalist. Sometimes, when the house was empty, she would retrieve the box and bring it into the living room and pore over her mementoes. Today had been one of those days; she had put the box back in its place just before it was time to pick up Lovisa and Tommy was due home.

Ingrid jumped when there was a knock on the window, deploying her parents' association smile before she had even turned her head and seen that it was Birgitta Nilsson, Lovisa's teacher. She checked the time involuntarily before rolling down the window.

'Doctor's appointment,' Birgitta said with a smile. 'Nothing serious, just a routine check-up.'

Ingrid liked her. She was approaching retirement age – Lovisa's class was going to be her last one.

'Good luck,' Ingrid managed to say.

'I saw Tommy on the box in last night's episode of *Agenda* – wasn't he good?' Birgitta clapped her hands together. 'So wise, so eloquent. You must be proud.'

'Very.'

'Not to mention that last autumn he took the time to come here and tell the class about his work, in spite of everything he has on his plate. When the other teachers heard he was coming, they were so beside themselves that we booked the main hall. Lovisa was so happy. Me too.'

'That's great. Yes, Tommy makes the time.'

The teacher reached in with her hand, patting Ingrid's shoulder before turning on her heel and disappearing towards the metro station.

Ingrid turned up the music.

She didn't really need confirmation of Tommy's infidelity. She already knew. He had been different since last summer. Placing greater emphasis on his appearance, suddenly hiring a personal trainer. Before, he'd felt able to discuss every single editorial decision with Ingrid in the room – he knew she'd never pass anything on and that she knew the rules. Now he was always making excuses and vanishing into the study or out into the garden.

'New policy from the owners,' he'd said by way of explanation when she had asked. 'And surely you're not interested in that stuff any longer anyway?'

But Ingrid wanted to know who the woman fucking her husband was. Probably someone on the paper – that was how they had met themselves. It was how journalists usually met.

Every day she would buy a copy of *Aftonpressen* and leaf through it at home. She barely recognised the byline photos any longer. Lots of her former colleagues had left the paper since her day, while others had left behind the toil of life as a reporter for management roles.

Did her old colleagues know that Tommy was betraying her? Did they feel sorry for her? Did they have his back – were they helping him conceal the affair? Ingrid had a plan for how to find out who he was cheating with, but she had no idea what she was going to do about it.

4. Victoria Brunberg

Malte and Lars were snoring. Their obese bodies secreted the smell of sweat and alcohol. Victoria took her husband's mobile phone down to the basement. She went into the box room where he kept his home still, grabbed a bottle of the transparent liquid and settled down on the plush couch in front of the switched-off TV. On the stand underneath it was his pornography collection, all lined up and in plain sight. She had watched every single one of them multiple times – that was how she had learnt Swedish. Malte was keeping her in isolation. The house had no internet.

Victoria had her own phone with a pay-as-you-go SIM. The hundred kronor that Malte topped it up with every month wasn't enough to call Russia. Victoria's only way to stay in touch with her mother was to hotspot the internet on Malte's phone to her own.

In the first few months, she had still imagined that life in Sweden might become passable. Not like the years with Yuri, but tolerable. Malte had been kind. Dull but kind. He'd brought home semi-wilted flowers, praised her for the food she had cooked, called her 'my little wife'. While it had been unappealing to sleep with him, have him close and feel his fumbling hands on her body, he had at least treated her like a human being.

She felt gratitude towards him for bringing her here from Russia. But after six months, he had begun to change. He'd become evil. He'd stopped showering. He smelled even worse. Instead of sleeping with her, he would yell 'blow job', pull his trousers down around his knees and sit on the sofa. And she obeyed and sucked his tiny penis. She was scared of him. While he might never have touched her physically, she was completely vulnerable to him. Malte could make her life even worse than it already was.

She had nowhere to go. The farm was a prison. If only she had a friend, someone who was actually kind to her and treated her like a person rather than a sex doll with added cleaning and cooking features . . .

She took a swig of the moonshine and grimaced. Her mother hadn't replied to her last email. Victoria was hiding her present situation from her. Lying and saying that she was fine, had loads of girlfriends and was happy. She said that Malte was spoiling her rotten; just like her mother had said Swedish men were, he was mild-mannered and kind and was a manager at a large IT company. She wrote evocatively about the splendid dinners, the trips to the Mediterranean, their powerful friends and the happy couple's plans to have children.

She thanked her mother for being so wise and considerate in suggesting a marriage in Sweden.

5. Birgitta Nilsson

In the waiting room at the small GP's surgery in the city centre, Birgitta Nilsson was still thinking about Tommy and Ingrid Steen. Wonderful people – both of them. Intellectual and full of humour. Their daughter, Lovisa, was so beautiful, the very image of her mother, while she had inherited her father's sparkling eloquence.

Birgitta tugged up the sleeve of her blouse and allowed her fingers to get to work on the eczema that had appeared on her elbow. Then she ran the palm of her hand over the tender rib on her left side. She had two years left until retirement. Her husband, Jacob, ought really to have retired already, but since he owned his own accountancy practice he wanted to carry on working. Sometimes Birgitta pretended that they were going to buy a house in Spain and live a peaceful, wonderful life of retirement together. That their twenty-year-old sons – twins Max and Jesper – would come down sometimes with their girlfriends to visit. She didn't really need a house in Spain. All she wanted in this life was love from the people she loved most on earth. She was so wrapped up in her own thoughts that she didn't even notice that there was a nurse standing in front of her saying her name.

'Birgitta Nilsson.'

'Good grief, please excuse me. I was a million miles away.'

Birgitta got up and followed the nurse down a corridor. At the end there was a door ajar. The nurse indicated with her hand that Birgitta should go inside.

'Thank you so much. And sorry, I'm getting old and confused,' she said apologetically before stepping inside the room.

The doctor was a handsome man in his mid-thirties. Black, combed-back hair, chiselled jawline and sumptuous lips. Birgitta proffered her hand and the man asked her to sit down. He cleared his throat, but Birgitta wasn't listening. She was looking at the framed photo on his desk. A beautiful, dark-haired wife, two small children with long thick eyelashes and mops of hair lying on a sandy beach and laughing into the camera lens.

'What a beautiful family!' she exclaimed in the middle of the doctor's exposition.

He fell silent and switched his gaze to the photograph.

'You must be so happy and proud. What angels – what an enchanting wife.'

'Thank you. Yes, truly. But if we could . . .'

The doctor pointed at the paper in his hand. Only now did Birgitta notice that he seemed troubled.

'Here I am, going on about trivialities. You're probably short on time, more patients waiting. You'll have to excuse me, I just babble on. Please, do go on.'

The doctor brushed back a dark lock of hair that had strayed onto his brow, and scratched his cheek. His kind eyes looked straight into hers.

'I'm afraid it's what we feared – you've got breast cancer.'

The doctor awaited her reaction, but it didn't come.

'Did you hear what I said, Birgitta?'

'Yes, yes.'

He leaned forward and covered her hand with his, looking her in the eyes. 'I can understand that you're shocked, frightened and worried. But the survival chances are good. We'll be in touch as soon as we've found a slot for the operation.'

Birgitta smiled at him.

'It'll be fine, my dear.'

She got up. Her chair scraped against the floor.

'Do you want me to call someone to give you a lift home?'

Birgitta shook her head.

'No, best not to bother them with this. I'll manage.'

The doctor muttered something, and Birgitta proffered her hand by way of parting.

'You had lots of letters telling you to come for a mammogram, but you didn't come?'

He looked at her searchingly. Birgitta smiled. She couldn't tell him the truth.

'I've had so much on, you know.'

She let go of his hand and left the room.

6. Ingrid Steen

Tommy was snoring heavily. Ingrid put her bare feet on the wooden floor, straightened her nightie and stood up. Taking slow steps, she left the bedroom and went downstairs. She picked up Tommy's coat, then the sewing kit, and headed for the bathroom, where she locked the door behind her. She quickly undid the stitching she had put in the evening before and put her hand inside. She removed the dictaphone. The light on it was still green; it was still recording. She stopped the recording and checked the light had gone off before emitting a sigh.

Ingrid stifled the impulse to play the content back right away. Instead, she sewed the fabric back together, unlocked the door and put the coat back in its place.

She put the dictaphone in the pocket of her own coat, headed into the kitchen and drank a glass of water. In a few hours' time, Tommy would be appearing on the breakfast news, while Lovisa was due at a friend's house for a playdate. She would have time to listen then. When she laid her head down on the pillow, she remembered how much she had hated listening to recordings as a journalist. Now she could hardly contain herself.

7. Victoria Brunberg

Malte was hung-over, his small eyes bloodshot and hostile. He was looking for faults, looking for something to correct or comment on. Victoria was making scrambled eggs. She set the frying pan down on the table beside the salt cellar and poured a glass of juice. He shook his head.

'Beer. Need to get rid of this hangover.'

She didn't reply, turning instead to the fridge where she retrieved one of the remaining beer cans from the day before.

'Anything else?'

Malte grunted. Victoria left the kitchen, put on one of Malte's jackets and a pair of wellies and opened the front door. The air was cold and sharp. She lit a cigarette. The field was grey, the sky was grey, everything was grey in this fucking country. There was a car driving along the road five hundred metres away.

She wished she had a driver's licence – or at least that she could drive a car. Then she'd be able to steal Malte's Saab and escape. Leave it all, go to Stockholm. That was where she had landed when she arrived from Moscow. She and Malte had stayed at a hotel, and he had taken her out for dinner in a fancy restaurant. Afterwards, at the hotel, she had realised that, as of then, she was his possession. She lived on his terms:

she was a walk-on in his life. She was expected to manage the household and part her legs in return for him providing for her.

The day after, they had gone to Heby and then into the forest before ending up in Sillbo. She had met Malte's parents. Over lunch at a pizzeria in Heby, they had stared at her as if she were an animal of some kind.

She had done her best to be polite; she'd asked questions in her broken English, but they had sat there in silence, staring. In the car on the way back, Malte had said that Swedes didn't like talking much.

Even if she had been able to escape, Malte had ensured by other means that she obeyed him. Without Victoria's knowledge, he had consistently filmed their sexual encounters over the first few months. He had said that if she disappeared, the films would be uploaded to porn sites. Including Russian porn sites. Victoria stubbed out the cigarette in a flowerpot and took off the jacket. The kitchen was deserted. Malte had gone down to the basement. She could hear the hum of the TV. Malte was shouting, unrestrainedly. Victoria cleaned up in the kitchen, washed up the frying pan, emptied the dregs of the beer down the sink and wondered what to do for the rest of the day. The fridge was almost empty. She would be forced to ask Malte to drive her to Heby to shop.

'Come here,' Malte yelled from downstairs.

Victoria closed her eyes. She knew what he wanted. She went downstairs.

'Blow job,' Malte said, his eyes glued to the TV as he pulled down his joggers and underpants. She knelt in front of the sofa and took his slack penis in her mouth.

He placed the beer can on her head and giggled.

'Fuck, why didn't I think of this before? Those feminist whores are right – women really can do two things at once,' he said, leaning back on the sofa.

8. Ingrid Steen

After dropping off Lovisa at her classmate's house and dutifully exchanging a few words over coffee with her parents, Ingrid piloted her silver Toyota Prius away from the suburbs and in towards Stockholm city centre.

She fast-forwarded through the recording until the point when Tommy had arrived at the newspaper offices. She drove aimlessly around the middle of the city, her white earbuds inserted into her ears. She held the dictaphone in her left hand, letting her wrist rest on the wheel as she made her way slowly down Sveavägen.

The morning stand-up meeting in Svante's office with the various bosses, a chat with a well-known, award-winning reporter about his latest series of reportage. A spell of silence. The sound of Tommy turning on his computer. Most of it was of no interest until what Ingrid calculated had to be lunchtime. His mobile phone rang – she heard him answering as he closed the door to the newsroom. His voice, initially formal, changed in character.

'Soon, sweetheart,' he said.

Silence. Ingrid held her breath.

'Oh right, so you're up for a long lunch then? Well, I've got a few things to do here, but see you at the usual place in thirty minutes.'

Ingrid came to a halt at a set of red lights close to the central station. A couple of pedestrians with wheelie bags crossed the street. A man in dirty clothing was digging through a dustbin looking for drink bottles with deposit returns. A woman was pushing a pram. Why was no one doing anything? Her world was falling apart and yet everything just carried on . . .

Behind her a car honked. The traffic lights had gone green. She pressed the accelerator, a little too hard. The car jerked and began to move. Her eyes on the road, she fast-forwarded exactly thirty minutes as she drove across the Centralbron bridge. The traffic was heavy – roadworks meant that only two lanes were open. Through her headphones, she heard Tommy walking through the newsroom, the dictaphone in his coat picking up the fawning remarks. Ingrid knew that he loved that. Tommy was a person who loved to feel important. Perhaps it was because he had grown up in a single-parent household, his father also a journalist. Ingrid had noticed early on in their relationship how sensitive Tommy was to flattery. Everyone was happy to be told they were clever and doing a good job, but for Tommy, that kind of external affirmation outshone everything else in life. That was how he had explained away the first infidelity. It had been a few months into her pregnancy with Lovisa. Ingrid had thrown him out, but after a couple of days she had forgiven him. He had promised it had been a one-time thing and she had believed him.

He got caught up in conversation with two sports hacks in the lift. Football. Ingrid could hear from the tone of his voice that he wanted to get out of there, that he was bored.

'You not coming to lunch with us then, boss?'

'Sorry, wish I could. But I've got a lunch meeting. Believe you me, I'd rather spend it discussing Serie A with you guys.'

Polite laughter. Apparently the idiots believed him. They didn't get that their boss was on the way to a lunch-fuck with his lover.

23

Silence in the lift. The doors opened. Tommy's echoing steps. Ingrid guessed he was in the underground car park. She tried to picture him in front of her, imagine what he was thinking. Did he have a guilty conscience? Was he thinking about her? About Lovisa? The car door opened. He got in behind the wheel. Ingrid jumped when another car door opened. Ingrid listened. Although nothing had been said, she was certain there was now another person in the car. For a second she thought she might be mistaken. Could it be a secret source that Tommy was meeting? She gazed out across the water at Söder Mälarstrand – across the boats moored there, looking sad and abandoned, awaiting the arrival of spring.

The next second she heard a zip being undone and Tommy groaning.

'You're quick off the mark today,' he chuckled.

'Since you force me to duck my head, I thought I'd make myself useful. How long have we got?'

'All the time in the world.'

Ingrid could feel herself getting dizzy. She glanced quickly in the rear-view mirror, pulled off to the right, removed her headphones and leapt out of the car. She rushed over to the wall and vomited into the dark water.

9. Birgitta Nilsson

Birgitta Nilsson was convinced she was going to die. She looked at the three men she had lived with for the last twenty-two years – the ones around whom her entire life had revolved. The twins, Max and Jesper, they'd have each other. Despite the fact that they were turning twenty-one next year, they still lived together, did everything together. She hoped they would take care of Jacob. He idolised and spoiled them. Jacob was a harsh and cold man – he had never shown her the tenderness she had longed for – but his love for their sons was uncompromising. It compensated for the coolness he displayed towards her – loving something together was as good as loving each other, she used to think to herself.

'How was work today, sweetheart?' she asked her husband, while passing a plate of boiled potatoes to Max.

Jacob muttered. He was still annoyed at the food being later than usual. Birgitta had hurried home from the GP and prepared food for the boys – as she called the three of them – but it had only been ready just after seven.

No surprise that they were quiet; they were starving.

They began talking about boats, which besides ice hockey was one of their favourite topics. Birgitta followed the conversation without participating. Jacob had been thinking about buying a boat for a long time and it was agreed that he and the boys would go together to Västerås to take a look at one that was up for sale.

'That will be fun for you,' Birgitta said.

No one answered.

When they had finished eating, they left the plates on the table and went into the living room. Birgitta scraped the remnants of food off them, cleaned up in the kitchen and put the leftovers in Tupperware. A red one for Jacob, and two blue ones for the twins to take back home to their flat. Their voices pacified Birgitta. The soundscape of her husband and sons in front of the TV was the setting that she had lived her life to since she had miraculously become a mother at the age of forty. She had done her duty, fulfilled her mission. The twins were grown-up, they could look after themselves.

Most things she said were met with indifference and she had stopped pretending otherwise. Sometimes she would daydream about the time when they had been little. Dependent on her and defenceless without her. Back then, they would creep into her and Jacob's bedroom at night. Sometimes the pain that those days were gone for good made her shudder. Afterwards she felt stupid. She couldn't help but feel envious of the parents in her class. They were living the best days of their lives.

Two hours later, Birgitta and Jacob stood side by side at the front door as they said farewell to their sons. They watched them disappear through the garden and head towards the bus stop before Jacob shut the door and turned to her.

'Why were you so late back?' he asked. His jaws were at work – chewing, grinding.

'Darling, there were parents' meetings and—'

The first blow landed – a clenched fist in the same spot it had got her last week. Birgitta fell over. He stared at her lying there. Still. Unmoving.

26

'If you weren't so fucking ugly, I'd suspect you were having an affair. But who'd want to fuck you?' he said.

Her gaze fixed on his right hand. The fingers were trembling. It was as if he hadn't decided whether there was going to be more. But Birgitta knew – she knew him well enough to know that there would be more. She had known it that morning. He had been taciturn, dogged. It was when Jacob wasn't shouting at her that she needed to look out.

Their sons' visit had merely postponed the assault. Jacob bent down and grabbed hold of her blouse. Birgitta closed her eyes. The blow came. All the air was expelled from her. She rolled onto her side, her face towards the wall as she heard his footsteps disappear into the living room.

Birgitta lay there for another minute or so, gathering strength, before bracing herself against the wall and laboriously getting up.

10. Ingrid Steen

Ingrid told Lovisa to occupy herself and brushed her teeth in the bathroom. She avoided meeting her own gaze in the mirror. She closed the toilet seat and sat down on the lid. Took a few deep breaths. Part of her wanted to carry on and pretend that nothing had happened. Hundreds of thousands, if not millions of women lived with unfaithful husbands. She knew Tommy had done it before, and she had forgiven him then. What would have happened if she hadn't? Lovisa would have been forced to grow up with parents who didn't live together. She would probably have gone back to journalism, rather than being at home all day, restless, feeling worthless.

She cleared her throat, got up and went into the kitchen.

Next to the huge stainless steel fridge there was an Apple computer showing her and Tommy's schedule. The idea was that the couple would note their commitments and appointments during the week to ensure they synchronised their weekdays. Tommy's colour was blue, hers was red. Nine out of the ten entries were Tommy's. Meetings, meetings, meetings. Galas, exhibitions, association of journalists meetings. Apart from three workout sessions, Ingrid's were all linked to Lovisa. Pick-up, drop-off, dance, football and homework. Next week, the only interruption to the pattern was a parents' meeting – green since it was a shared activity. Tommy had stoically offered to attend.

She clicked the schedule off the screen in irritation and opened the browser. She googled: *unfaithful husband what should I do?*

11. Victoria Brunberg

They parked outside the sleepy ICA supermarket in Heby. The sky was grey, rain lingering in the air. People in tracksuits were dragging carrier bags towards their rusty cars. Victoria went inside and collected a trolley.

'Hurry up. And no unnecessary crap – I'm not a millionaire,' Malte muttered.

No, that you most definitely are not, Victoria thought to herself.

Malte walked in front of her. The T-shirt, too short, combined with his grey joggers, too low-slung, meant that his arse crack was staring her in the face. He didn't care. He greeted acquaintances he encountered with a reserved 'hello' or a nod.

By the time they had reached the milk, Malte had begun to sigh and had crossed his arms ostentatiously when Victoria caught sight of Mi – Lars's Thai wife. The small woman smiled widely. It was as if someone had stabbed her from ear to ear.

She was always happy. What was her problem? Was she happy in this hellhole with these sluggish, insolent farmers?

'Heeyyy, Victoria, how are you?'

Victoria smiled stiffly back at her and replied to the cheery greeting. Malte and Lars had also found each other. Their booming laughter echoed throughout the store.

'I'm making noodles tonight. What you making?' Mi asked cheerfully, peering down into Victoria's trolley and picking up the items to examine them.

Cyanide and broken glass pie, Victoria thought to herself.

'Potato hash,' she replied. She didn't even have it in her to smile.

Lars and Malte came walking towards them. Malte had his arm around Lars's shoulders.

'We have to celebrate, so fuck this,' he said, gesturing towards the food in the trolley.

Victoria looked at him quizzically.

'Lars is going to be a dad,' Malte said, thumping his friend on the back.

'Mi told me this morning,' Lars explained with pride.

Victoria sighed silently. Of course it was nice to get away from the house – the outing to Heby was hardly an odyssey of happiness, but it did offer a break in the monotony. But now she would be forced to put up with an afternoon and evening at the pub in Heby.

'So we're not shopping now?' she asked.

'Fuck me – is it beyond you to be a little happy and spontaneous?' Malte bellowed. 'Didn't you hear what Lars and Mi said? They're going to be parents. We're going to celebrate.'

'I have to go home to change. You too,' Victoria said, pointing at the stained joggers.

'Pfft. I'll borrow a shirt off Lars. Right, mate? And you can wear one of Mi's dresses. That'll be fun, won't it?'

Victoria eyed the small Thai woman, who returned her frozen gaze with a smiling thumbs up.

12. Ingrid Steen

Ingrid was sitting at the kitchen table watching the movement wash over Sweden, over the world – starting with the USA. #MeToo was everywhere.

Ingrid's Facebook feed was full of women standing up, telling their stories and shouting. Rape, sexual assault, control. Everyone had something to tell. Everyone. It was hypnotising. She couldn't stop reading the stories. She went over her own life. Her teens in Västerås. Years when she had barely given a thought to being called a 'whore' if she turned down an admirer at the pub. Nights when she had got hammered at some party and woken up without her pants and with fragmentary memories of hands on her body. That was assault. And it didn't stop there. The early years at the paper. Female colleagues who warned against ending up alone with certain reporters and photographers. Their male colleagues who laughed and smoothed things over when someone was too pissed and their wandering hands pinched arses, breasts and waists. The crime correspondent who, when she had proffered a hand to introduce herself at the start of her first week of work, had looked her up and down and instead of saying his name had said *what incredible cock-sucking lips*.

The assaults had been part of the game for so long, but now the rules of the game had changed.

Ingrid put down her mobile phone and got up. She went to Lovisa's room to check that her daughter was asleep. She adjusted the duvet, pulling it over Lovisa just as she heard the sound of Tommy's car. He walked up the drive with hurried footsteps. Ingrid closed the door to Lovisa's bedroom and went downstairs. Tommy took off his shoes, caught sight of her and shook his head.

'Fuck me, what a day . . . I have to be in the newsroom at seven tomorrow morning. Again.' When Ingrid didn't reply, he continued, 'Sensitive publication. Bloody sensitive. The final version of the article is coming in half an hour.'

They went into the kitchen. Ingrid brewed them coffee while Tommy sat down at the table.

'Two female employees came to see me today. They want the paper to fire Ola Pettersson and Kristian Lövander. Apparently they've been misbehaving.'

'Surely you knew that already?'

Tommy smiled faintly.

'Yes, but it's not like they mean any harm. They're old guys from another era. This equality thing is new to them. Neither of them can pass up an opportunity for a few drinks. They don't behave like that because they're bad. Anyway, we need them on the paper – they're respected journalists with resumés no one else can match. Readers trust them. Bloody hell, Lövander looked after me when I joined the paper. I can't fire him.'

'What did you say to the women then?'

'I said I'd look into the matter and asked them to keep it in the family, so to speak.'

Ingrid felt uneasiness spreading through her body. Two young women had come to Tommy and asked for his help, but he had turned them away and gagged them.

'Tommy, you've got to—'

He fixed her with a glare.

'I don't have to do shit. You don't understand what's best for the newspaper. For us.'

'But—'

'Shut your trap. Jesus! I'm not in the mood. You haven't a clue what you're talking about.'

Ingrid fell silent. They drank the remainder of the coffee in silence and then Tommy got up and headed for the stairs. Ingrid cleared away the empty cups and washed them by hand.

13. Birgitta Nilsson

There was a cold wind but the sun was shining and the water was glittering at Vinterviken. Birgitta Nilsson lit a cigarette and carefully sucked in the smoke, stifling a cough and then exhaling. She took a long swig from the Coca-Cola bottle. Fizzy drinks and nicotine were the tastes she associated with the Aspudden neighbourhood she'd grown up in. This was the place that had shaped her identity.

Once a year she would come back, stroll between the apartment blocks and round off her tour by sitting down by the rocks at the shore with her Coke and ciggies.

She had never said anything to either Jacob or the boys, and no one had asked either. She shifted position and felt her ribs aching.

Why didn't you come for your mammograms? the doctor had asked. Birgitta smiled and let out a laugh. She took another drag on the cigarette and checked that she had gum with her to conceal the smell.

How surprised he would have been if she'd straight up told him why.

Because my husband beats me to a pulp whenever he's in the mood. He hits me in places where you can't see it. And I usually think that if it's not visible then it doesn't exist.

She had been twenty-seven when she had met Jacob at the pub in the Klara neighbourhood, still referred to by that name despite having been demolished long ago. She couldn't remember the name of the bar and it didn't matter, come to that. Jacob had come in with a few friends. A recently graduated accountant in a brown suit, with slicked-back hair and a slim necktie. A snob, she had thought to herself. One of his friends had come over to Birgitta and her friend and invited them to join the finance bunch. They'd said they'd think about it, and a while later they'd stumbled over. Jacob had been taciturn even then. Introverted. While his friends had kept the conversation going, he had calmly sipped a glass of wine, interjecting with the occasional comment. Later on, the same evening, the party had moved on to a nightclub. Birgitta hadn't enjoyed the loud volume. Jacob had tugged her arm and asked her whether she wanted to go on somewhere else where it would actually be possible to hear themselves thinking.

'Are the others coming?' she'd asked.

Jacob had shaken his head.

'No, just you and me.'

She had felt chosen. Special. She had realised that Jacob was a man who didn't waste unnecessary words. There and then, she had become his. There and then, her life had changed. If Birgitta hadn't gone with him it might all have been different.

Two children in colourful snowsuits with big hats jammed down over their brows were skimming stones at the water's edge. Birgitta looked around to see whether there was anyone keeping an eye on them. There could so easily be an accident. There was a young woman sitting on a bench watching them play. Birgitta nodded. At the same time, part of her was disappointed. What if the children had gone into the water and she had had to rescue them? She couldn't think of a more beautiful ending than sacrificing her life for two children. Maybe even the twins and Jacob would be proud of her then and say lovely things about her in the newspaper.

'You're losing your marbles,' she muttered to herself.

14. Victoria Brunberg

The pink dress she had borrowed from Mi was far too small and slipped up her behind whenever she made the slightest move. Victoria was constantly on her guard to avoid showing her most intimate parts to the rest of the patrons at the pub in Heby.

They had secured a table for four. The men had positioned themselves opposite each other. Victoria was curled up on an uncomfortable chair with the incessantly nodding and laughing Mi across the table from her.

The leathery meat and soggy fries had been eaten. Malte ran a finger over the plate to mop up the last traces of bearnaise sauce.

'Right, let's drink! Well, not you, Mi. That'd make the kid deformed and slow,' Malte exclaimed, raising his beer glass and revealing his yellow teeth. The corner of his mouth and his cheeks were glistening with shiny fat. Mi's hysterical laughter cut through Victoria like a knife.

'Bloody hell, cheers!' Lars added, before downing the contents of his beer glass and calling over the server to get more.

During the first months, Victoria had been the one who had kept conversation going with Malte, the one who had tried to get them to find points in common. She'd kept him happy and satisfied. That time was over. She was increasingly struggling to disguise her contempt. She couldn't understand how Mi managed to keep her spirits up. The little Thai woman laughed and nodded at every single idiotic comment to emerge from the mouths of Lars and Malte. She seemed satisfied with life in Heby, satisfied with having an obese husband who never washed and spoke about her as if she were some kind of pet. Was there nothing else behind the laughter and those empty eyes?

'Want to come to the ladies with me?' Victoria asked.

Mi nodded.

They got up. Victoria quickly pulled down the dress so that it at least covered the top half of her buttocks. The men in the pub leered without any embarrassment and licked their lips. While they were standing in line for the toilets, two older Swedish women glowered at Victoria.

'Imported whores,' one whispered to her friend, nodding towards them. Victoria threw an angry look at them and then glanced at Mi, who seemed altogether unmoved.

The women disappeared.

'Doesn't it bother you that they talk about you like that?' Victoria asked Mi as she settled onto the toilet seat.

Mi seemed surprised.

'No?'

Victoria sighed and pointed at her belly.

'Are you happy?'

'Very. Lars also happy. I want to make him happy.'

'Don't you hate this fucking place?'

'Heby?'

'Yes.'

'Heby's nice.'

'But don't you miss your home country, your family, your friends?'

'I didn't have a family. I had nothing. Here, I have everything.'

Victoria sighed and pulled down her dress. Mi opened the door and contemptuous eyes focused on them as they made their way into the corridor. In Ekaterinburg she would have clawed out the eyes of women who looked at her like that, and no one had ever dared to. Not after she'd met Yuri.

Victoria had been working in a lingerie store in an exclusive shopping mall in the city centre. One afternoon, Yuri had come in accompanied by a beautiful woman and two bodyguards. The platinum blonde had been all dolled up and had wrinkled her nose and waved Victoria away when she offered to assist.

She had taken lots of exclusive lingerie sets into the fitting room, and Yuri had winked at Victoria. A little later, the woman had emerged from the fitting room and nonchalantly slung the lingerie onto the counter. Yuri had got up from the armchair and handed over an American Express card. In his hand there had also been a small note with a smiley and a phone number on it.

Once they had gone, Victoria had looked over the digits and realised they were her big chance in life. Although she was glad she had a job, it was boring serving dull millionairesses in return for wages that barely covered her rent and groceries for the month. She had seen men like Yuri in the nightclubs of Ekaterinburg, spending more in a night than she made in a year. Their women could barely walk for all the diamonds and gold jewellery weighing down their slender bodies. Somewhere inside herself she had always known she would become one of them, and since Yuri could hardly take his eyes off her she realised this was her chance. But her visit to Ekaterinburg's gangster society couldn't be a brief excursion – men like Yuri changed women on a monthly basis. No, she had to play her hand right. It took four days before he came back. Since his first visit, she had spent ever more time in front of the mirror in the morning. This time he came without Ivana and with just one bodyguard in tow. He had a carrier bag with him. His eyes fixed on Victoria, he came over to the till and held up the bag.

'Wasn't it to your satisfaction?' Victoria asked with a teasing smile. She pulled out one of the thongs and held them up. 'It takes a real woman to wear these. I'm afraid underwear is non-returnable. You'll have to ask your wife to be more careful when trying them on.'

'You didn't call?' Yuri said.

'Call?' Victoria looked surprised. 'Who are you saying I should have called?'

Yuri grinned.

'Have dinner with me. Tonight?'

'Dinner or not, you still can't return the lingerie. Sorry. Store policy.'

'I don't give a fuck about the underwear. I want to see you.'

'I'm working. As you can see.'

Victoria felt her heart pounding. Was she playing too hard to get? She was about to say she accepted when Yuri reached for his mobile.

'What's your boss's number?'

Victoria gave him the number. She heard him introduce himself using his full name. She heard her boss's surprised voice and then Yuri turned around and walked away a few steps with the phone glued to his ear. After a minute or so he came back towards her.

'Okay, it's a deal. I'll ask my lawyer to send over the contract. Goodbye.'

Yuri hung up and put his phone back in his pocket.

'I've just bought the shop. New opening hours now apply. You get off in five minutes.'

* * *

41

Victoria was drawn out of her memories by Malte abruptly elbowing her.

'They're not doing table service any longer. Get two beers,' he said, pointing towards the bar.

15. Ingrid Steen

Tommy hadn't turned up for the parents' meeting like he had promised he would. Instead, Ingrid was seated awkwardly on one of the small school benches while Miss Birgitta, as she was referred to, sat opposite her.

Ingrid could barely think straight after the conversation with Tommy. How could he display such a lack of empathy? Women on his own paper had been terrorised by those two hacks since time immemorial. And no one did a thing about it. Instead, Tommy sat on the sofa on TV breakfast shows going on about equality, patting himself on the back for bringing a woman onto the editorial team. He was a hypocrite. Ingrid was an even bigger hypocrite for backing him up.

'Should we wait for the editor-in-chief?' Birgitta asked, glancing towards the door.

'That won't be necessary. I'm afraid duty called and he couldn't get away from the paper today,' Ingrid said mechanically. How many times had she heard herself say the same thing over the past year? Why did she continue to protect the cheating bastard? Maybe the old biddy wanted to join Tommy's harem?

'What a pity,' Birgitta said. 'But of course I understand. He's doing an important job, what with all the terrible things going on in the world at the moment.' Ingrid didn't reply. Birgitta hadn't finished putting Tommy's excellence into words. 'I read his column on Sunday. He writes with such dignity. Passion.'

Ingrid had to make an effort not to roll her eyes. Instead she squirmed, making the chair legs scrape the floor.

'Shall we get started?'

'Of course, dear,' Birgitta said, clapping her hands together. She quickly scrutinised the paper in front of her. 'Little Lovisa takes after her wise father and her beautiful mother. She is superb in all subjects and . . .'

Ingrid got into the car. She couldn't let this carry on. She had to do something. The anger was bubbling inside her. She got out her phone and sent a text message to the babysitter, asking her to stay another two hours. Without waiting for an answer, she headed for the *Aftonpressen* newsroom in the city centre.

After doing laps for a few minutes hunting for a parking spot, she got bored, pulled into a loading bay and switched off the engine. She walked straight through the swing doors and was heading for the revolving door when she realised she didn't have a pass. She turned around and approached the solitary receptionist.

'I'm here to see the editor-in-chief of *Aftonpressen*. Tommy Steen.'

The receptionist nodded.

'Do you have an appointment?'

'I'm his wife.'

The girl behind the desk smiled apologetically.

'I'm sorry, everyone needs to have a pass or an appointment. Those are the rules. Maybe you could call him and ask him to come down and fetch you?'

Ingrid leaned forward and fixed her gaze on her.

'You're going to open the door now. Get it?'

The woman opened her mouth but at that moment Ingrid

heard her name being called out. She spun around. One of her former colleagues, Mariana Babic, pulled her into a warm embrace.

'Here to visit Tommy?' she asked.

'I thought I might.'

'Pity. I was hoping you were making a comeback, but then you'd already have a pass. Come with me.'

Mariana tapped her pass card on the reader twice and let Ingrid in. While they were in the lift together, all Ingrid could think about was whether Mariana knew about Tommy's affair. They'd arrived at *Aftonpressen* at the same time, spent time together regularly, including outside of work, and now Mariana was political editor and one of the top bosses at the paper. Ingrid felt inferior, passive and lost while Mariana cheerfully peppered her with questions. Was that an undertone of pity in Mariana's face?

The lift doors slid open and they got out.

'No need for me to show you where his office is, right?' Mariana said with a chuckle.

'I'll find it.'

Mariana looked at her seriously.

'It would be . . . We should meet up some time. If you'd like?'

'Sure,' Ingrid said, though she knew Mariana was only saying it to be kind.

'Well then, it's a deal. See you.'

She leaned in and hugged Ingrid again before disappearing along the corridor. Ingrid began to head towards Tommy's office. She recognised some of the faces she passed, quickly greeting them but not stopping. She passed the culture desk and went straight past the central desk – the heart of the paper.

Tommy's glass-walled office was positioned to afford him a view of the newsroom. He was sitting, deep in concentration, with his feet on the desk as he wrote on the laptop perched on his lap. She knocked and stepped inside. He looked up in surprise – few of his employees came in without waiting for an answer.

'What are you doing here? Is Lovisa okay?'

'Yes, don't worry.'

Ingrid closed the door behind her while Tommy sat upright and pushed away the computer.

'Then what are you doing here?'

Ingrid settled down in one of the two visitors' chairs.

'What's going on with Ola Pettersson and Kristian Lövander?' she asked.

Tommy looked at her searchingly.

'How do you mean?'

'The accusations made against them are serious.'

'Why the hell are you storming in here to discuss that? I thought I made myself clear at home the other day.'

Ingrid turned her head and looked out into the newsroom. Then she turned back to Tommy.

'At my first summer party, Ola Pettersson stuck his hand up my skirt and said that one of my duties as a temp was to be "test driven" by him. He was forty. I was twenty-three.'

Tommy stared absently at her but didn't react. She wondered how he'd propositioned the young reporter she'd heard sucking him off in the car. Maybe she'd already passed her on her way in.

'He's an idiot, but—'

'But what, Tommy? He's an idiot but he's won Journalist of the Year so it's okay for him to touch up young girls' cunts? And did they give Kristian Lövander the Golden Pen so that he could tell female temps that pussy was part of his salary package?'

'Calm down. You know that's not what I mean.'

'Then what do you mean?'

Tommy sighed. He ran the palm of his hand over the stubble that had grown on his cheeks in the last few days.

46

'Fire them,' she said. 'How the hell can you report on the misdemeanours of celebrities if you don't set your own house in order?' she said, clenching her fist and taking a deep breath. 'Jesus, you're such a fucking hypocrite. Nothing but a weak, fucking hypocrite. That's what you are,' she shouted.

Tommy recoiled. 'What the hell's wrong with you? Calm down.'

He threw a worried look over her shoulder and waved at someone walking by with feigned cheeriness.

'If those two bastards haven't got the sack in the next forty-eight hours, then I'm taking it to *Sveriges Nyheter*. They'll probably devote a whole show to it if I share my memories of Ola Pettersson's exploits – on the record, with my name and face.'

'You'd never do that,' Tommy said. She could see his face turning red. A second later he exploded. 'You can't be that fucking disloyal! You'd be hurting the paper. You'd be hurting me.'

He got up so quickly that the chair he'd been sitting on fell over with a crash.

Loyalty? Who was he to talk about loyalty? The hypocrite! Ingrid opened her mouth to yell that she knew all about his infidelity, but changed her mind. She clenched her fists and took a deep breath.

#MeToo. The rules of the game had changed, and she had to play smart. Tommy was still standing there, glowering at her. His face was bright red.

'I want those whoremongers off this paper in forty-eight hours,' she said calmly, getting up.

She was shaking with rage as she left the office. She walked through the newsroom, her gaze set dead ahead, without acknowledging anyone.

16. Victoria Brunberg

Malte was snoring beside her. Every single pore in his heavy body was secreting a suffocating stench of alcohol. Victoria put her feet on the floor, opened the window even further, then got back under the duvet. Three minutes later she got up again. Malte would sleep late into the next day. If she took the car, drove to Stockholm and then took the ferry to St Petersburg, he wouldn't be able to find her. All she needed was her passport and a few thousand kronor for petrol and the ferry ticket. She could make it to some small seaside town on the Baltic where no one knew her, get a job in a shop, start over . . .

Anything was better than being Malte's house pet.

Victoria crept into the hallway and went downstairs. She looked around. Malte kept the valuables in a small safe, which should be where the cash was too. Her heart was pounding hard in her breast. She felt exhilarated, full of energy.

She was getting out of here. Finally. She began to hum the Russian national anthem as she fished the keys out of the flowerpot and caught sight of the dark fields outside covered in thick fog.

She went to the safe and unlocked it. Her burgundy passport was at the very back and there was three thousand kronor in an envelope. She took the cash and put the passport in her jeans back pocket. She put on a thick coat and looked around the hallway. There was nothing else she would need – she didn't want any souvenirs from this house.

The car keys were usually left on a hook in the hall. Victoria felt for them with one hand – but there was nothing on the hook.

17. Ingrid Steen

Ingrid stared at the woman on her laptop.

She had gone to the *Aftonpressen* TV website to watch the latest round-up of news on #MeToo and suddenly – that voice. The same voice that had been giggling in the recording from Tommy's car. No: the same lips that had been sucking his cock. Ingrid froze the image and leaned in. The presenter, Julia Wallberg, was blonde, had large green eyes and lips that were made for advertising ice cream. She was incredibly beautiful. And young. How young? Ingrid headed to Wikipedia. Twenty-five. Her career had been meteoric and she had been named as one of Sweden's most important decision-makers under thirty. Hadn't Ingrid glimpsed her earlier in the day at the newsroom? No, she was imagining it. Ingrid found Julia's Instagram: 22,000 followers. Photos in studios, at the pub, outside cafés during the summer.

A photo from Palma. Tommy had also been there in July, along with a childhood friend. Ingrid got up and checked the calendar on the computer by the fridge. They had been there at the same time. How long had the affair been going on? She scrolled back up through the Instagram feed. Her eyes widened when she saw that, just a few seconds earlier, Julia Wallberg had posted a new selfie at the Taverna Brillo Italian restaurant.

Ingrid raced upstairs and checked that Lovisa was asleep, then she went into the bathroom and hurriedly made herself up, changed into a smart top. Sitting downstairs was one of the neighbour's teenage girls with a bowl of popcorn, her eyes glued to her mobile. She'd babysat Lovisa before, and it had been easy to tempt her over with the promise she'd pay twice the going rate. Ingrid didn't want to run the risk of Lovisa waking up and finding herself alone. She had an idea of where Tommy might be. Ingrid waved, grabbed her coat and locked the front door.

18. Victoria Brunberg

Twenty minutes later, Victoria still hadn't found the car keys. They weren't in any of the coats or in the chest of drawers by the front door. She took a deep breath. Might they be in Malte's jeans in the bedroom? He was definitely sound asleep, but she didn't want to tempt fate.

She pressed down the door handle and squinted into the darkness. The warm stench of beer and sweat hit her. She took off her shoes.

'The last time,' she mouthed in Russian, walking as quietly as she could. Malte was snoring. Her eyes quickly adjusted to the darkness – the big pair of jeans was hanging over a chair by the window. She felt the fabric carefully with her hand. The keys fell to the floor with a thud. Victoria jumped, stood stock-still and held her breath. She glanced over at Malte, who had stopped snoring. He murmured something. Was he still asleep or was he awake? The spent, stale air burned in her lungs. Victoria opened her mouth and exhaled it as quietly as she could. She inhaled fresh oxygen and bent down. She touched the wooden floorboards with the palm of her hand, found metal and cupped her hand around the keys.

She squeezed them hard to ensure they didn't jangle. Then she sank down almost onto her stomach, grimacing, and crawled along the foot of the bed, heading for the door.

19. Ingrid Steen

Ingrid hung her handbag and coat on a hook under the bar and ordered a gin and tonic. Taverna Brillo was full of trendy young people in hip clothes. Julia Wallberg was sitting at one of the round tables together with two girlfriends. She was wearing a white blouse and navy skirt. Occasionally, someone would come up to them, exchange a few words and then wrap up by taking a selfie together with Julia. She was laughing – she seemed to be having fun. She was friendly to the people who came up to her – even if Ingrid couldn't hear what was being said.

Shielding her phone screen with one hand, she opened the browser and googled Julia's name. She might as well make use of the time to do some research. The problem, she realised, was that she didn't actually have a clue what she'd do next. Confront Julia? Ask her how she could have the brass neck to be drawn into an affair with a married man?

Julia Wallberg, she read, had been born and raised in Borås, but had moved to Stockholm to study at the Kaggeholm Folk High School. Alongside her studies, she'd run a YouTube channel on politics, and that was what had caught *Aftonpressen*'s attention. She lived on Bergsunds Strand in the Hornstull neighbourhood.

Her hands were shaking. Ingrid looked up, letting her gaze linger on the young woman while she took a sip of her drink. Did she know what Ingrid looked like? Time to find out. She checked her hairdo in the mirror, grabbed her bag and coat and got up. She passed Julia's table with her eyes looking dead ahead.

She was holding her iPhone discreetly pointing towards the group. She ducked to the left and went into one of the toilets. She shut the door. Took a deep breath. Her heart was pounding, her legs shaking. Her hands trembling, she played the video back. She smiled when she saw Julia's reaction: the young journalist's eyes had opened wide and she had elbowed the friend next to her and nodded towards Ingrid. Ingrid sat down on the toilet seat and squeezed out a few drops while considering her next move. She had been out of the house for two hours; it was just after eleven and she really ought to go home. But for some strange reason, she wanted to be near Julia. She discreetly exited the toilet, and returned to the bar by another route – just in time to see Julia parting from her friends. Ingrid waited for thirty seconds before following her outside.

The rain was pouring down.

Outside the main door, Ingrid began to run towards the car, which was parked by Humlegården. Just as she leapt in behind the wheel, there was a beep on her mobile. She turned the key in the ignition, pulling out onto Birger Jarlsgatan as she read Tommy's message.

Are you at home?

She smiled. Julia had been in touch with Tommy. Told him that she'd seen his wife out on the town.

As she manoeuvred the car towards Kungsgatan and towards the Centralbron bridge, she composed her reply.

Where else would I be?

Ingrid smiled, put the phone on the passenger seat and concentrated on the road. The windscreen wipers were working frenetically to deal with the downpour. With a little luck, she'd make it to Julia's front door before she did.

20. Victoria Brunberg

Victoria took a top and a pair of trousers out of the dirty laundry basket and put them in a plastic bag. The clothing was wrinkled and smelled a little musty but a change of clothes would come in handy. She didn't dare root through the wardrobe in the bedroom. She took two tins of tuna from the larder, chucked a can opener in the bag and filled a plastic bottle with water. The money she'd taken from the safe was all she had – it had to stretch as far as possible.

She looked around in the darkness. Had she forgotten anything? She carried her boots in her hand to avoid making any unnecessary noise and headed for the door that led into the garage. She carefully opened the door, bent down and laced up her boots. She didn't have a licence, but Yuri had taught her to drive. A BMW rather than a shitty old van – but still. It would probably be fine. Once she was behind the wheel, she squeezed the button on the garage door remote. The strip of light from the courtyard widened in front of the bonnet. Victoria was about to start the engine when she saw a movement diagonally behind her. The door from the house had opened. Malte. It had to be Malte.

'What the fuck?' he yelled.

She fumbled the key, got it into the ignition and turned it. The engine spluttered into life just as Malte wrenched open the driver-side door.

21. Ingrid Steen

The rain continued to pour down. Bergsunds Strand was practically deserted. Ingrid had double-parked twenty-five metres from the door to Julia Wallberg's building, but the young journalist still hadn't turned up.

Maybe she'd been wrong? Maybe Julia wasn't done for the night. Maybe she was going on somewhere else? Ingrid remembered how on certain occasions in the past she herself had showed up in the newsroom straight from the pub.

Her thoughts were interrupted by a man turning onto the street carrying a large red umbrella that concealed his face. For a moment, Ingrid was convinced that it was Tommy, but the man passed the door and her car and carried on towards Långholmen.

Ingrid switched on the engine, kept the headlights off to avoid drawing attention to herself and raised the temperature inside the car. She blew warm air onto her frozen hands. What was she going to do when Julia showed up? And what if she wasn't alone – what if she was with Tommy? Would she get out and confront them? Scream, cry? Curse their betrayal, Tommy's lies . . .

Two people were walking along the street from Hornstull, entwined beneath a large umbrella. Tommy and Julia. Ingrid stared. Her grip on the wheel tightened. Ingrid was hyperventilating. She released the handbrake, put the car into first gear and accelerated towards them.

Around her, the building facades were shooting past.

Tommy and Julia crossed the street at the crossing – they hadn't yet spotted the car racing towards them with its headlights off.

22. Victoria Brunberg

Malte threw his enormously fat body over hers and tried to reach the key in the ignition. Victoria floored the accelerator, but the vehicle didn't budge an inch. The handbrake was still engaged.

Malte got there first. He shouted and pounded his fist against Victoria's breast. She roared, trying to bite his back. Eventually, he managed to get hold of the key and wrenched it out. The engine fell silent.

He withdrew from the car. He rested his hands on his knees, breathing heavily. Victoria rested her head against the steering wheel. She had been so close. So terribly close. After a minute or so, she could feel him spitefully contemplating her.

'I thought you were a thief who had got in,' he said, still trying to catch his breath. Victoria didn't answer. 'Were you just going to leave?'

Victoria glowered angrily at him.

'I don't want to stay here. I want a divorce. I miss home.'

For a second, Malte looked surprised – as if he were going to suddenly take her hand, pat it and say 'I understand'. But the quizzical expression was quickly replaced by one of anger.

He straightened his back, took a step forward and grabbed Victoria's arm. He wrenched her out of the cab.

'You spoilt fucking whore,' he bellowed, throwing her towards the back door. 'You were going to bail? Leave me after everything I've done for you?'

His eyes glaring, he came up to her and pressed her neck against the van with his forearm. Victoria gasped for air.

'Please, please let go,' she hissed.

She felt the world spinning, red dots dancing inside her retinas. Victoria realised she was going to die.

'I've been too kind to you,' said Malte, looking her right in the eye.

Victoria tried to reply, to apologise, but she couldn't manage to summon the words. All that came out of her mouth was a gurgle. The next second, she lost consciousness.

23. Ingrid Steen

They were going to be thrown up onto the bonnet and they were going to die. And she was going to drive away from there, turn right onto the bridge heading towards Liljeholmen, and disappear. It would look like a hit-and-run. A random drink driver who had ended the lives of *Aftonpressen*'s editor-in-chief and a rising television presenter. As the car rushed towards Tommy and Julia, Ingrid could picture herself in the church, wearing black and a veil, receiving condolences with dignity.

The speedometer said she was doing seventy-three kilometres an hour – there was about twenty metres to go.

Tommy looked up and froze. Julia's mouth formed into a scream.

At that moment, Ingrid realised her mistake. The satnav. How many true-crime podcasts had she listened to where the murderers' alibis had crumbled because of technology? Even if Ingrid told the police she had been at home and she scrubbed the car free from all blood, they'd still turn over every stone. Not least when it turned out that Tommy was with his lover. She'd go to prison. At the last moment, she turned the wheel a few degrees to the right.

The car skidded, missing Tommy's body by a few centimetres.

Ingrid straightened the car up. The wheels got a grip on the slippery asphalt and she sped up. In her rear-view mirror, she could see Tommy and Julia watching the car go.

Now he knew she knew.

How was he going to react?

The traffic light was red, but there were no other cars in sight. Ingrid turned right, heading for Liljeholmsbron bridge. She wondered whether he would call or wait until they saw each other. Would he stay at Julia's to calm down, plan his next move? And what was she meant to do?

Get divorced? Apply for jobs in journalism? Digitisation meant she'd hardly be an attractive prospect on the labour market. She didn't even have Twitter. But Ingrid would have to support herself. The prenup was as clear as day – she wouldn't get a penny of Tommy's money in the event of a divorce. Would he leave her and start a new family with Julia? She was young – probably wanted kids. Ingrid overtook a truck without indicating and pulled back into the inside lane. No, divorce was out of the question. No matter how she looked at it, Tommy had to die. For what he had done to her and to ensure that she and Lovisa avoided the shame of wasting away in some rented flat in a distant suburb.

24. Birgitta Nilsson

In the attic was a doll's house that Birgitta had played with as a girl and that she had planned to give to the daughter she had never had. When the twins had been little, she had still brought it down from the attic so they could play with it. But when Jacob had got home from work he had flipped.

'Jesus Christ, do you want to turn them into queers?' he'd shouted, tipping the doll's house onto its side. Birgitta had had to hurry to put it back in the attic, otherwise he would have smashed it into kindling. Instead, he took the boys out into the garden with a hockey stick each.

Birgitta ran her hand over the roof of the miniature house. Once it had become clear she wasn't going to have a daughter, she had decided to give it to her grandchildren. But now it was unlikely she'd have time to become a grandmother. That was a pity. She was convinced she would have been a good grandmother – at least, better than the mother she had been.

Birgitta patted the doll's house one final time and cautiously went downstairs. She was still a mother. Her responsibility for the boys wasn't over yet. It was up to her to make sure they had a good life even when she was gone. Without the financial handouts from Jacob they got every month, they wouldn't make ends meet. And truth be told, it was getting more expensive to keep them afloat. Jacob's accountancy practice, which appeared to be successful and respected on the outside, was on its knees. Birgitta knew he had 'borrowed' money from clients to invest in various projects. The returns from those projects had not materialised. Instead, some of the investments had made losses. It was only a matter of time before it was discovered. Then Jacob would be in a tight spot – he'd probably end up in jail. Birgitta could have lived with moving out of the house, living in a flat – cutting expenses so that they could give the boys a couple of thousand kronor every month. But now? She was going to die, and Jacob was going to be prosecuted. Poor boys.

They could have solved it by signing over their properties and cars to Birgitta or the boys to protect their assets, but Jacob had refused. Now it was up to Birgitta to solve it all. And quickly too.

She took the bus to the school, went down to the library and switched on one of the computers. She logged in with a guest ID and went to Google.

25. Victoria Brunberg

There was a rattle when she tried to speak. Her throat was strained and hurt – a bit like when she'd had tonsilitis as a little girl. It even hurt to cry. The night before, she had been convinced she would die with Malte's fingers around her throat.

Before she had been knocked out, she had asked herself how many women in history had ended their lives with that exact same sight: the man they had married, a contorted expression on his face, looming above them while the life was squeezed out of them. When she had come to on the cold stone floor of the garage, she had taken deep breaths of the petrol-laden air. She had lain there for two hours before she had got up on shaky legs and staggered into the house.

She had promised herself not to become one of those women. Malte would never get the chance to end her life. No man would ever get that. But she needed help.

26. Ingrid Steen

It took three days for Tommy to show his face at home. Up to the moment he stepped through the door, Ingrid spent all her time polishing the plan that she had hatched.

When she heard the front door opening, she stayed where she was, sitting calmly at the kitchen table. Tommy popped his head into the kitchen, looked at her and then came slowly into the room.

Stay calm, Ingrid thought to herself. Everything depends on you staying calm.

Tommy pulled out a chair. Carefully, as ever, lifting the legs a couple of centimetres off the floor to avoid making a racket. He sat down, fixing his gaze on Ingrid. She waited a few seconds. She had promised to love him for better or worse, until death parted them – and she intended to keep that promise.

Tommy cleared his throat.

'How long have you known?' he asked.

'A couple of weeks,' Ingrid replied quietly.

'Why . . . why didn't you say anything?'

'What was I supposed to say, Tommy?'

'Something. Anything. Instead you tried . . . to kill me,' he said, shaking his head slowly.

'I didn't mean to kill you. Or her. I was just so upset. Angry.'

'And now?'

'Now I'm mostly upset.' Ingrid ran a fingernail over the table. 'Are you going to leave me?'

Tommy extended a hand and placed it on hers. It was big and warm. Small islands of straggly hair were growing just above the knuckles. Before, when they had been younger, she had helped him to wax those.

'I don't see how we can get through this.'

Ingrid squeezed the hand.

'Lovisa needs you. *We* need you,' Ingrid said, steeling herself. 'You can't leave us now. Be with her if you must. I can understand that I've not been easy to live with.'

Tommy blinked, uncomprehending.

'You mean that you're . . . that it's okay?'

Ingrid nodded.

'As long as that's what you want. But keep it tidy, so that no one finds out. I can live with it if it means you're still here for me.'

Tommy struggled to hide the fact that he felt like he'd just won the jackpot.

Poor bastard, Ingrid thought to herself. The poor, pathetic wretch of a man.

PART 2

Three weeks later

27. Ingrid Steen

Ingrid parked in the car park outside the old garrison. She turned around. Lovisa was fully occupied with her iPad.

'I'll be back in a minute,' she said.

She opened the car door and checked there were no traffic wardens nearby. A group of schoolchildren in neon yellow vests passed by. Ingrid opened the door to the post office, letting an elderly lady walk slowly out while she examined the roof. No cameras so far as she could tell. It didn't really matter. She was just there to retrieve an envelope from a PO box. Box 1905. The same as the year Norway had declared independence from Sweden. She ducked right and stopped in front of the long row of metal boxes. Ingrid was about to take off one of her leather gloves, but she changed her mind. When she found the right box, she got the key out of her bag and inserted it into the lock. Turned it. Inside were two envelopes, but she returned the one that said *Three* on it in old-fashioned handwriting. Ingrid was number two – both last month and this time.

She wondered who the other two women were. Best not to think about it too much. Just like her, they probably had their reasons, she thought to herself.

Lately, Tommy had been away for two or three nights a

week. She wondered how he had explained the arrangement to Julia. She must think Ingrid was desperate, letting her husband have an affair. Perhaps they were laughing at her. It made no odds.

She put the envelope in her bag, locked the box again and left the small post office. Lovisa barely looked up when Ingrid opened the door and slid in behind the wheel.

'Time for us to go home, sweetheart.'

'Is Dad coming home tonight?'

Ingrid shook her head.

'No, not tonight. But he promised he'd be home tomorrow.'

28. Birgitta Nilsson

Lying inside the boot of the hire car was a five-metre length of wire and a can of black spray paint. She had also bought a basic toolbox including a screwdriver and hammer. For Birgitta it felt like she was driving around with a bomb or a couple of kilos of coke. She had been careful to stick to the speed limit all the way from Stockholm. Even so, she had checked her rear-view mirror every three seconds, expecting to see the blue flashing lights at any moment. The letter – which she had burnt after reading it twice – was written in halting Swedish. Just like the first, heartrendingly desperate cries for help that she had stumbled across on the Family Life online forum.

While she might be about to kill a man, she was also going to liberate a woman. The sum of her actions would be a positive. And then someone was going to liberate her. She enjoyed the feeling of freedom – it felt good to drive a car without anyone commenting on her driving. Jacob only let her drive when he was tired. He had even opposed her getting a licence in the first place.

She passed a petrol station, stopped at a crossroads and then drove past a sign marked Heby. To her right there was an ICA supermarket.

'Right after ICA,' she repeated to herself. She peered into the darkness, found the turning and indicated. She left the small community behind and found herself enveloped in dark forest. The road was narrow. When she encountered the first car, she wasn't sure whether the roadway was wide enough for them both. The other car passed by uncomfortably close. Fifteen kilometres, then the sign would appear.

She hoped that the woman she was going to save had done her part. Otherwise someone might get hurt. Someone innocent. Birgitta didn't know what she'd do with herself if that happened. She could feel her palms getting sweaty and she wiped them on her thighs. The time was 16.37. She put her foot down as much as she dared in these slippery conditions. It was better to arrive too early than too late. She hoped it would be easy to find the place and that the unknown woman's instructions were precise.

29. Victoria Brunberg

Victoria was pacing back and forth in the kitchen. She wished she had a cigarette left, but she had smoked them all already. She had gone over the plan a hundred times. Things could go wrong – horribly wrong – but she had to take the chance. Malte had to die and if Victoria was going to avoid spending the next few years in prison, then this was the only way out.

She had done what she could do; now it was up to the other person, who ought to be nearby by this time. The trees were discreetly marked. The car was in the garage, unusable, and in a minute or two Malte should be putting on his helmet and climbing onto the motorbike. Hopefully he would take the shortcut through the forest, just like he did every time he took the motorbike. As long as it didn't start raining. She'd heard the furious profanities coming from the garage. When he stormed into the house, Victoria thought he'd looked at her suspiciously. She was imagining things. She knew Malte didn't think she was capable of ruining a car. A bit of sugar in the petrol tank and it was all done and dusted. Just like her mother had instructed her when her good-for-nothing classmate Aleksandr had touched her up at the youth club disco in her early teens. The blue moped that he'd been so proud of had never started again.

30. Birgitta Nilsson

The trees in the forest were creaking in the wind. The darkness was dense. Using a torch, she had found a red scarf tied to a tree trunk. Birgitta looked around, got the bag out of the boot and shook the can of spray paint. She was about to apply the paint to the wire when she realised she was standing too close to the car. No traces, she thought to herself. Then she shut the door and walked a few steps away. She made quick work of the task with the spray paint. The fumes left her a little dizzy and she giggled. When she was done she shone the torch on the wire and noted with satisfaction that it didn't gleam at all.

'Good.'

She checked her wristwatch – there were only a few minutes left until the man was supposed to show up. She had thought she'd wait until the last minute so that no one else got hurt. On the other hand, she realised that it was unlikely anyone else would come driving this way. No sane person would get on a motorbike of their own volition in this weather.

She strung up the wire, gave it an experimental tug and then went back to the car to drive off.

She pulled at the handle. Locked. She groped in her pockets. Nothing. The keys weren't there.

'No, not now. Anything but that,' she gasped.

31. Victoria Brunberg

Victoria ran through the checklist in her head once more. She noted, again, that she hadn't forgotten anything. As long as her unknown saviour did their part and Malte was as predictable as usual, she would never see him again.

She got out the ingredients she needed to make meatballs and mash and went over to the cooker. In Russia, she had dreamt of becoming an actress and joining a theatre company, but she had dropped out before her first play when it had become clear she wasn't being given the leading role.

Now, in a few hours' time, her talents as an actress would truly be put to the test. And then she would be free.

32. Birgitta Nilsson

Birgitta felt the panic welling up. Where could she have dropped the key? She turned around and jogged back the way she had come, shining the torch on the ground.

'Please, please,' she whispered.

Could she call it off? Take down the wire, go home and forget all about it? The other women didn't know who she was, so they would never find her. But then she wouldn't be rid of Jacob. What would happen to the twins when she was rotting in her grave? They weren't strong enough, weren't ready for life. Birgitta returned to the car and shone the light through the window. The keys must be inside. She looked around for a rock, pointing the torch at the ditch beside the track. There. She picked up the rock, weighed it in her hand and took aim, drawing back her arm and lobbing it with all her might at the passenger-side window. It exploded in a shower of glass shards.

There was a gaping hole right in front of her.

The next moment, she heard the sound of a vehicle approaching.

She twisted round to look. On the larger road, a single light source slowed down and turned towards her.

She threw one final, helpless glance at the hire car before

taking a few steps across the ditch and into the forest. The sound of the engine grew in intensity. She lay down behind a stone, breathing heavily, seeing the road in front of her illuminated. She couldn't see the wire, but the rider was approaching the two trees.

Just a few metres to go. Birgitta closed her eyes. When she opened them she saw the motorbike disappear into the forest and crash into a tree and fall silent. She craned her neck, trying to understand what had happened to the rider. Was he alive? The forest was silent. Her footsteps echoed as she made her way through it.

The wire had come off.

She followed the tyre marks a little way down the track before they deviated off into the forest.

He was lying in front of a tree. His body was contorted, legs and arms at unnatural angles like a stick man drawn by a small child.

'Good God,' Birgitta whispered. 'Good God.'

She slowly approached him, fumbling for her mobile phone with trembling hands. She found it, fiddled with it for a bit to turn the torch on, and then gave up. She shone the feeble light of her display on the driver.

A small movement of his arm made her realise he was still alive. Blood was dripping from beneath the bottom edge of the helmet onto his top. She moved the light downwards. She screamed. A large tree branch was sticking out of his chest. Birgitta put her hand to her mouth to silence herself. She had to get out of here. Quickly.

Twenty minutes later, Birgitta was panicking. She had got the torch on and shining it in front of her she had searched everywhere inside the car for the keys. Now she was forced to acknowledge they weren't there. She lay down on her tummy, sweeping the beam of light under the car. Could she leave on foot? Impossible. The car hire company had her name. The police would ask why she had left the scene of the accident. She could say she had lost her mobile and gone for help. No – far-fetched. Far too far-fetched. They would be able to see that the mobile was in the area and switched on. But she couldn't stay there until the police arrived. Or was that exactly what she should do? She glanced at the car, trying to marshal her thoughts. If she was found at the scene of the accident without having contacted the police it would look bad. She gave it some thought for a while before dialling 112 for emergency services on her mobile. She stood at the feet of the body, crouched, reached out with an arm and opened the visor. Dead eyes stared out into nothingness. There was a click on the phone.

'Help,' she wailed. 'Help me! He's dead!'

The female voice on the line was calm and authoritative. 'What's happened?'

'An accident. A terrible accident.'

33. Victoria Brunberg

She quickly went over to the open window and listened. Silence. She saw the silhouette of the forest beyond the fields but could see nothing moving. She checked the time. Malte was dead. He had to be dead. For a second she was struck by panic. But she forced herself to pull herself together. The meatballs were sizzling. The smell of cooking in her nostrils brought her back round. Everything should seem just as normal. She left the window open and went to the cooker. She took hold of the frying pan handle and shook it back and forth a few times. The police would turn up sooner or later. When they did, she would need to play the loving and considerate wife. How did someone react when they were told that their beloved was dead? She – of all people – ought to know. But she had no idea – she couldn't remember the hours after Yuri had been gunned down.

Had she spoken to anyone? Cried? Screamed? All there was inside her head were a few blurry images of her throwing herself over his body. Seeing the blood pumping out of the hole in his chest, holding his head and watching as the life drained out of him. Around her, there had been people screaming in panic, tugging and trampling all over each other to get out. He had been staring up at the ceiling. But what about her? Victoria didn't know. She took the lid off the pan, the steam burning her wrist. Malte's potatoes were ready, but he would never eat again. She hadn't done anything wrong, she was a good wife who had been waiting at home with her husband's favourite meal. The next moment she heard sirens and she rushed to the window. There were blue lights flashing in the forest.

34. Birgitta Nilsson

She went and waited by the bigger road. When the police car was approaching – according to her watch exactly thirteen minutes after she had called 112 – she waved at it frantically. The siren stopped. Two serious-looking police officers, a man and a woman, looked at her gravely. The man had his hands on the wheel. His window was rolled down. Birgitta pointed into the forest.

'In there. He's in there. Oh my God, it's so awful.'

'You'll have to come with us and show us,' the policeman said authoritatively.

Birgitta nodded. Her heart was pounding, creating an absolute storm in her ribcage. She opened the back door and got in. They pulled off the road onto the small forest track.

'Oh, thank God you came. I didn't know what to do. I think he's dead. It's so horrid. Poor man, the poor man.'

The police officers were serious and taciturn. The policewoman turned around and scrutinised her. The woman's expression was equivocal. Did they suspect her? She asked them to stop a couple of metres before the wire and they got out. The engine of the patrol car was still running, illuminating the forest. The policewoman's gaze was caught by the hire car.

'Is that your car?'

'Yes. It's my car. I . . .'

'It's okay. Show us where.'

Birgitta went ahead of them into the forest.

'There he is, the poor thing. I can't understand – what could have happened?'

The police officers went up to the man and whispered to each other. The woman put her hand to her shoulder and said something into her radio. Birgitta looked around nervously into the darkness. It felt ominous. She was guilty of murder and right now she was standing here lying to two police officers. But in their eyes she was just a confused primary school teacher. A witness who had done her civic duty and called the police.

'You can go back and wait by the car.'

It was the policewoman again.

'Can I leave?'

'No, we want to talk to you. I'll come over in a little while.'

While she waited, she tried once again to find the car keys but without any joy. Her mobile phone battery level was glowing red. There wasn't much juice left. She opened the back door and got in without closing it behind her. She left her feet resting on the gravel outside the car.

The policewoman came walking towards her, followed by the policeman. Birgitta put her head in her hands and leaned forward. They stopped in front of her.

'Are you okay?' the man asked.

She liked him better; he seemed softer and less on his guard than his colleague.

She nodded and theatrically gulped a few times.

'What's your name?' he asked, crouching in front of her.

'It's . . . Mona.'

'Your car . . . the number plates have been removed and the window's smashed.'

'I know,' Birgitta whispered.

87

'What happened?'

'I had a break in earlier today. In Sala.'

She looked up. The policewoman was shining her torch towards the tree where Birgitta had strung up the wire.

'Olaf, look at this,' she said, heading for the tree. 'It's a wire. A fucking wire.'

The policeman got up, got out his gloves and put them on. They leaned in and examined the wire before returning to Birgitta. She made an effort to look dumbfounded.

'So it wasn't an accident?' she whispered. 'Is that what you're saying?'

The police exchanged a look before the policewoman spoke.

'We don't know that. What did they take?'

'Who?'

'During the car break in.'

'My handbag and the number plates.'

The policeman went over to the hire car and shone his torch through the window. The light danced on the car for a while before he returned. Birgitta tried to read his facial expression. Was there something that didn't add up? Did they suspect her?

She cleared her throat.

'Did you report the break in to the police?'

Birgitta shook her head, trying hard to look unhappy.

'No, not yet. I was going to tonight when I got home.'

'Do you live nearby?'

'No, in Stockholm. I was in Sala to visit my sister Gunilla. She's sick – in hospital. And it was there – the hospital that is – that they struck. I just wanted to get home.'

The policeman's gaze softened slightly and he put a hand on her shoulder. She looked up and smiled at him.

'What are you doing here then? If you were heading for Stockholm?'

'I took a wrong turning.'

'For twenty kilometres?'

'I've never had much of a sense of direction, I'm pretty scatter-brained. I was going to stop in Heby for a bite to eat, but I missed it and then I didn't dare turn on this narrow lane. I pulled in here – in the forest – to try and turn around. And it was then that it happened.'

There was a crackle on the police radios and they each held up a hand in a synchronised move. They listened. Birgitta wiped her sweaty palms on her trousers.

'So you saw the accident?'

'No, but I heard a dreadful sound. I have to say I was terrified, but I thought someone might have got into trouble, so I got out of the car and that was when I found him.'

'Have you got any ID?' the policewoman asked.

Was that a hint of suspicion on her face? Birgitta shook her head – was it worth trying to squeeze a few tears out?

'It was in my handbag that they stole,' she said disconsolately. 'I just want to go home to my husband. What a day! What an awful day. I don't know how I'm going to teach those poor kids tomorrow. Perhaps I'll have to call in sick. I'm a teacher, you see.'

'But have you . . .'

The policeman put a hand on his colleague's arm.

'Excuse us for a moment.'

They walked a short distance away. Birgitta couldn't hear what they were saying, but they seemed to be in disagreement. She glanced towards the hire car. The number plates were wedged under the chassis. She hadn't dared throw them into the forest in case they were found when day broke. Her handbag and the spray paint were under the front seat. If they searched her car, they would soon realise she had put up the wire. The officers came back again. The policeman kicked something. He bent down and picked up something between his thumb and forefinger.

They were too far away for her to see what it was.

'I think these must be yours,' he said, coming towards her.

Birgitta wanted to vomit – what on earth had they found? She squinted towards him. There was a flash of metal in his hand. The car keys.

'I must have . . . oh my God. Thank you, officer. I must have dropped them when I went to wait for you on the road.'

He handed over the keys.

'Just leave us your name and phone number and you can go,' he said with a smile. The policewoman looked unhappy, standing there with her arms crossed a short distance away.

Birgitta gave them the name of her childhood best friend Mona. She took her leave. The policeman escorted her to the car.

'Will you be all right getting home?' he said before she shut the door.

'Yes, I should think so. I'll drive slowly. Thank you, officer.'

She closed the door and put the keys in the ignition. The car started up and Birgitta got ready to pull away. But at that moment there was a tap on the window. She jumped and fumbled with the button to lower it.

'Don't forget to report the break-in,' the policeman said.

35. Victoria Brunberg

There was a ring at the doorbell. Victoria checked the dinner preparations one last time and then wiped her hands on the apron she had tied around herself in honour of the day.

She opened the door and made an effort to seem surprised. The two police officers looked at her grimly.

'Hello,' she said haltingly.

'May we come in?'

Victoria nodded and stepped to one side. The policeman pulled the door shut behind him and introduced himself as Olof Lönn. He pointed to his female colleague and said:

'This is my colleague Lisa Svensson.'

Victoria noticed that they were glancing over her shoulder towards the kitchen where dinner was on the table. Olof Lönn took off his gloves and ran a finger over them. He hesitated for a while. Victoria felt sorry for him.

'There's been an accident nearby. The victim is a man, Malte Brunberg.'

Victoria shivered. She stared at him. Olof Lönn swallowed and shook his head.

'Is he going to make it? Will Malte be okay?'

'I'm afraid not. He's dead.'

'Are you sure it's Malte?'

'I'm afraid so. We found his driver's licence. And the motor-bike is his.'

'Is it okay . . . I mean . . . Can I sit down?' Victoria asked, gesturing towards the kitchen table.

While Olof Lönn held her by the arm and gently helped her to a chair, his colleague filled a glass with water and set it down in front of Victoria. She took a few hesitant sips.

'What happened?'

The police officers exchanged looks, then Olof Lönn spoke again.

'We're not quite sure. Do you know whether there's anyone – a neighbour perhaps – who puts up wires?'

'Wires?'

'Yes, cable. Between the trees.'

Victoria put her hands to her mouth.

Then she explained: around a week ago, Malte had bought a wire from a hardware store. He'd been sick of the youths who sometimes sped down the tiny forest track. She had tried to dissuade him and said that someone might get hurt. It was probably illegal, she'd said. But Malte had refused to listen.

'Why did he take the motorbike this morning? The weather isn't exactly ideal.'

Victoria looked up. It was the first time Lisa Svensson had opened her mouth.

'I don't know. He loved that motorbike. Even when he was only going to work. I told him so often that he should drive carefully. Especially now that it's cold. But Malte didn't listen.'

A tear trickled down from the corner of Victoria's eye.

'But if he had put the wire up earlier this week or yesterday, surely he would have had to take it down when he went to work this morning?'

Victoria pretended to think for a while.

'The mailbox. It's on the main road. Malte usually picked up the mail on his way to work. He must have gone that way this morning.'

She reached for a napkin.

36. Ingrid Steen

Ingrid Steen looked around, put the keys in the door and breathed a sigh of relief when they fitted. She went into the foyer and studied the sign with the list of surnames. Julia Wallberg lived on the top floor – the fifth floor. Ingrid sighed. She didn't like lifts. But that couldn't be helped; she would have to hurry. Lately she had been forced to do things she didn't like at all.

She got into the lift and pressed the button. Tommy's gloves were far too large, but she knew she would have to keep them on. Fibres or even the odd strand of hair being found in Julia's apartment could be explained away by the affair. But a fingerprint was, on the other hand, completely out of the question. No.

What she was about to do went beyond her wildest fantasies. To start with, her revenge had only been aimed at Tommy. It was as if her rage grew with each passing day. And as that rage swelled, so her own imagination expanded.

She got off at the top floor and noted it was quiet. Five minutes. No longer. Ingrid carefully opened the letterbox and peered through it. Dark. She straightened up and unlocked the door and went inside the apartment. Unfamiliar smells hit her nose. For a second she hesitated. Perhaps she should turn back, leave and be satisfied with what was waiting for Tommy . . .

Ingrid turned around to leave the apartment, but as she did so her eye was caught by the coat hooks. There was one of Tommy's jackets.

'You bastard,' she muttered.

She went into the apartment. The parquet creaked. The living room faced towards the water, while across the channel loomed Liljeholmen. The walls were decorated with black-and-white fashion photographs. Marilyn Monroe seemed to be Julia's favourite subject. The blonde was smiling. The blonde was smoking. The blonde was looking horny. 'So predictable,' Ingrid murmured. 'I'm disappointed in you, Julia. I thought you were more exciting than that.'

She opened the bedroom door. There was a large bed with a substantial headboard. She was immediately overcome by images of what Tommy and Julia got up to there. Ingrid quickly closed the door and returned to the living room. She would need to find somewhere that Julia didn't check regularly. Ingrid went over to the TV unit and opened it. There were a few magazines and a DVR. Two photo albums. She resisted the temptation to leaf through the albums, reminding herself of what she had come to do. The TV unit would have to do. Ingrid reached her hand into her handbag and pulled out a small bag. Five grams of cocaine. She hid the bag under the magazines at the back of the unit before changing her mind. She turned around, found the bathroom and went in. Standing in a glass by the sink there were two toothbrushes. She grabbed them and rubbed the bristles against the bag. She couldn't magic fingerprints out of thin air, but plenty of DNA ought to do the trick.

The fall of Julia was just a bonus. She could deal with her later, once Tommy was dead. She left the little bag on the side, spun around and grabbed the toilet brush. Ingrid carefully rubbed the toothbrushes against it. 'No kisses for you for a while, Tommy boy,' she said, putting the toothbrushes back and then returning to the living room.

Getting onto the metro at Hornstull, she messaged Tommy. *You dropped your keys on the driveway.*

37. Victoria Brunberg

The train pulled into Stockholm Central. Victoria Brunberg had only been to Stockholm once – with Malte, in their earliest days together. She enjoyed being absorbed into the anonymity of the crowds as she got off the train. She was no mail-order bride, she was no one at all. Just one of thousands of people.

She had two days. First she needed to buy a suitable dress – according to the instructions in the letter, she would have to go to a cocktail party on a boat. Her client had allocated her three thousand kronor for this purpose. It wasn't the same level as the clothes that Yuri used to spoil her with, but Victoria was longing to dress up and make herself beautiful after the years with Malte. She stopped in front of a taxi sign and headed left towards the rows of waiting cars.

The sky was light blue, a weak sun shining without any warmth.

A driver waved her over right away, put her bag in the boot and held the rear door open for her. Victoria got in.

'Grand Hotel, please,' she said.

He confirmed this with a nod and pulled away.

Of the man Victoria was going to kill she knew little, but the woman who had signed his death sentence probably had her reasons – just as she had with Malte. Victoria was on the guest list for the party. Not in her own name, but as Natasha Svanberg. The instructions on what she should do then were set out in detail.

Victoria took out the small passport photo of the man. He was smiling slightly. He had bright, kind eyes and a chiselled jawline. Judging by appearances, he was neither cruel nor evil, but she of all people knew that a photo could hide a man's true nature.

If Victoria could share the feeling of freedom she'd experienced herself since Malte's death, then she would more than happily follow the instructions in the letter.

The car pulled up in front of a beautiful building by the water. Across the water, Victoria recognised the royal palace. She paid, and the driver opened the boot. Even before her bag had touched the ground, a man in livery hurried to her side and offered to take it.

'Thank you,' said Victoria with a smile.

'After you,' the man said formally.

38. Ingrid Steen

Tommy was snoring beside her. Ingrid reflected that it was their last night together. She felt, surprisingly enough, indifferent. No regrets, no qualms of conscience. Inside her was nothing but indifference. Perhaps it was biological: the man she had chosen to reproduce with because he would defend her and their mutual offspring had betrayed her. Left them unprotected.

Tomorrow he would die at the hand of an unknown woman. But that wasn't all. His reputation as an honourable, hardworking journalist would be crushed. Before long, all of Sweden would know what a dishonourable remnant of a man had been heading up Sweden's biggest tabloid. The reporters Ola Pettersson and Kristian Lövander, who he had refused to do anything about, would look like choirboys beside him. It would be obvious to everybody why he had protected them.

Ingrid sighed and turned away from Tommy's back.

She needed to sleep. Tomorrow would hardly offer her any rest. She would have to get up earlier than Tommy to prepare his breakfast. In the evening, she had arranged for her mother to babysit Lovisa. As soon as Lovisa had been dropped off, she would be heading for a restaurant where she could be certain of being seen.

She was going to get away with both the murder and the character assassination of Sweden's best-known editor-in-chief.

39. Victoria Brunberg

After quickly popping up to her room to drop off the bag containing the black dress and the short, white fur coat she had bought, Victoria got in the lift to go back down to the bar.

She noticed how she drew appreciative looks from the male hotel guests. Victoria sat down in a leather armchair and a waiter in a white shirt immediately appeared by her side.

'Vodka, please,' she said, without looking at either him or the menu.

'Ice?'

She shook her head. While Victoria waited, she opened the newspaper lying on the table in front of her. The editorial was about the #MeToo movement. Victoria hadn't read a newspaper since last summer and she was hypnotised. The next article, a long cultural piece, was about how men in positions of power exploited young women.

After reading the introduction, she looked around for the waiter before quickly noticing that the vodka was already there on a napkin in front of her. She took a big swallow.

The next moment she almost spat out the spirit. She coughed. In the middle of the piece was a photo of the man who was going to die.

She blinked and stared.

There was no doubt about it. It was the same person.

Aftonpressen's editor-in-chief Tommy Steen insists the newspaper is taking accusations of sexual harassment against two male employees seriously, the caption explained.

Later on in the article, Tommy expanded on his reasoning, explaining that he couldn't act until the men in question were found guilty of anything. He also responded to criticism that he had not named the employees as he had done with other men working in other industries.

Her palms felt clammy, and she took another large swallow of vodka and put down the newspaper. Tommy Steen was his name, and he was the editor of the paper she was holding in her hand. She oscillated between dread and excitement. The waiter stopped by her table and cleared his throat discreetly.

'From the gentleman over there,' he said, nodding towards a handsome man in a dark suit standing at the bar.

In the ice bucket covered in condensation that the waiter set down on the table was a bottle of Moët & Chandon. She flashed a dazzling smile at the man and the waiter began to open the bottle.

40. Ingrid Steen

Ingrid mechanically reached out to switch off the alarm clock on her mobile before it had gone off for more than a couple of seconds. She felt wide awake and rested.

Tommy mumbled to himself as she wrapped herself up in her dressing gown and padded out of the bedroom. Hanging in the hallway was the change of clothes for Tommy to wear in the evening. Under the pocket square was a small bag containing two grams of coke.

In the kitchen, she switched on the coffee maker she had set up the evening before. She glanced at the calendar on the computer.

20:00. MS Ocean Star.

The international media conglomerate which, in addition to *Aftonpressen*, owned two TV channels and dozens of other publications in Sweden, had chartered the majestic vessel for their annual company party. Since the weather was mild and the waters around Stockholm still ice-free despite it being December, they were going to take a trip out into the archipelago, if Ingrid had understood correctly. When Tommy had dutifully invited her, she had – to the relief of both of them – said no. But that hadn't stopped her from having Natasha Svanberg added to the guest list under Tommy's name.

She could hear water flowing through the pipes. Tommy was always quick in the shower.

She put out a mug, poured some coffee, mixed in a bit of the leftover cocaine and stirred it with a teaspoon.

Then she poured herself her own cup of coffee and got out her iPad.

41. Victoria Brunberg

The thick curtains prevented any light from penetrating. The suite was in darkness, the furniture a series of dark shadows. Lying next to her was Al, as the tall American was called. He was breathing heavily without snoring. His hair, which had been so neatly swept into a side parting the day before, was plastered to the crown of his head.

Victoria checked her mobile – it was quarter to nine in the morning. They couldn't have slept for more than three or four hours.

The American, Alan DePietro, was a businessman working in oil, and had lived in Russia for several years.

As a result, they had quickly switched to Russian after he had approached and asked whether he could join her. He was polite, charming and urbane. Al treated her with caution – with respect. After staying in the bar until closing time, he invited her up to his room. At first she said no. But when Al made no further attempt to persuade her, paid the bill and wished her good night, she changed her mind.

'Is there any vodka?' she asked, laughing.

The suite was almost at the top of the hotel and comprised three rooms in a row. There was an ample terrace overlooking the palace. It was the most incredible hotel she had ever seen.

She felt like Julia Roberts in *Pretty Woman*. First, Al had let her order whatever she wanted off the room service menu. An entire dinner had been served to them on beautiful silver platters out on the terrace. Stockholm had slept as they ate and drank while swathed in blankets. Al was almost twice her age – approaching fifty. He had told her stories of Texan oil barons and Russian oligarchs he had met that Victoria had only seen on TV. She urged him to tell her about their homes, their boundless luxury and private jets.

But in addition to entertaining her with anecdotes from a long and exciting life, he listened to her, appreciated her views and described her thoughts as 'interesting'.

Afterwards, when they were freezing, Al had fired up the sauna. They had brought the champagne into the bathroom but never made it into the sauna. Instead they had sex in the shower, quickly towelled off and then picked up where they'd left off in the big bed.

Victoria kicked the duvet off, went to the window and pulled the curtains apart a crack. A feeble beam of light split the room in two. On the nightstand was an empty bottle and two champagne flutes.

Victoria gathered up her clothes, put them on and padded towards the door. It was a pity they'd never see each other again.

'Natasha?'

She stopped mid-movement. She hadn't used her real name. She had invented some story about working in a clothes shop, and now she regretted it.

At least the bit about the name.

'I thought I'd let you sleep,' she said.

He waved her over and Victoria perched on the edge of the bed.

'While you were snoring your head off, I did some thinking,' Al said with a smile. 'Like I told you, I've never had a family, and I celebrate every Christmas by getting hammered in some hotel where the staff are paid an obscene amount of money to keep poor bastards like me company. This year I've booked an all-inclusive resort in Barbados.'

Victoria waited patiently for him to continue, but had to do her best not to crack a big smile of delight.

'What I'm suggesting is that you come with me to Geneva today, or later in the week and then celebrate Christmas with me in Barbados? Stockholm is great, but the weather isn't the best . . .' Al said, with a gesture towards the window.

'I don't know. I'd been thinking I would go home to Russia. To my mother.'

Al smiled, but Victoria could tell he was disappointed.

'I understand,' he said, patting her hand. 'Pity though.'

42. Birgitta Nilsson

For the first few days, Birgitta Nilsson had spent every waking moment expecting to hear a knock on the door from police officers who'd come to put her in handcuffs and take her away. But the police, questioning and trial never came. Instead, before she returned the hire car she took it to a garage and paid for a new window to be fitted.

The pain in her body was growing worse; fatigue became a state of normality. Nevertheless, she ignored the letters summoning her for treatment. Birgitta was done with life. She was staying alive in the knowledge that Jacob was going to die and that she had to be there for the twins. But she didn't want to embarrass them, didn't want their father to be exposed as a wifebeater. As soon as he was gone and the bruises had healed, she would begin chemotherapy. Jacob's assaults had increased, become more raw, more consummate. He didn't hit her to hurt her but to repair himself. He struck blows mechanically without showing any emotion. And Birgitta took it without displaying any emotion. Perhaps that was one of the things that provoked him and made him hit harder.

She bade the class a good afternoon, gathered up her papers and gave the classroom a quick tidy before locking up.

The corridor was almost deserted. Only Lovisa Steen was still there.

'Anything the matter, my dear?' Birgitta asked.

'No, nothing.'

'You sure?'

The girl nodded.

'Then why are you still here?'

'Mum's picking me up a bit later today, and then I'm going to Grandma's.'

'How lovely! Is she nice, your grandma?'

Birgitta helped her to put her large backpack on and they walked side by side past the rows of coat hooks.

'Mum and Dad are getting divorced,' Lovisa said suddenly. The girl bit her lip.

Birgitta started. Tommy and Ingrid Steen? Bromma's most perfect couple? Well, what did anyone know these days?

Tears appeared in Lovisa's eyes.

'There, there, sweetheart,' said Birgitta, leading her to a bench, sitting down with the girl on her lap and hugging her. She didn't know quite what to say.

They sat in silence.

Birgitta felt a tear on her hand.

'I've got cancer. I'm going to die,' she whispered.

She realised the moisture was coming from herself.

43. Victoria Brunberg

Victoria reached the pier just a few minutes before the MS *Ocean Star* was due to sail. Two bouncers in black wearing thick coats scrutinised her with uninterest, asked for her name, checked a list and then nodded before letting her past. Her stilettos echoed off the gangway as she boarded. Through the windows she could see that the partygoers had wasted no time. Festivities were already under way and music was booming across the almost-deserted deck. A few plucky smokers were satisfying their nicotine cravings while fighting the cold. Victoria opened the door and stepped inside. The men were wearing dark suits, most of them with open collars. The women were in party frocks. She avoided making eye contact, aimed for the bar at the back of the room and made her way over to request a glass of white wine. She looked around, searching for Tommy Steen, the man she was going to kill. Opposite the bar there was an elevated area – on the small stage was a microphone stand, two guitars, a bass and a drumkit.

A man in his sixties with thinning hair got onto the stage with a glass of champagne in his hand and used the tip of his index finger to test the microphone. The hubbub fell quiet and faces turned towards the man.

'My dear colleagues, welcome aboard. We're about to set sail on a voyage through the archipelago . . .'

Victoria stopped listening, allowing her gaze to sweep the room again. The speaker produced a volley of laughter just as Victoria spotted the editor-in-chief of *Aftonpressen*. He was standing nearby, diagonally to Victoria's right, beside a young woman. Both Tommy Steen and the woman seemed to be listening with interest.

They were standing close together, slightly too close together for them to just be colleagues who had ended up side by side. Every now and then the woman would put her hand around his, quickly but openly, and squeeze it. There was no doubt that there was something going on between them. Might she be the one who had sent Victoria here and ordered the murder? If so, she was ice cold. And crazy.

'Cheers!'

The man on the stage raised his glass towards the gathered masses.

Victoria put her lips to her glass and took a small sip. She didn't want to drink too much. She needed to stay sober, even if she would have preferred to numb her nerves with more alcohol.

The room was filled with applause. Victoria set down her glass and joined in. The man got off the stage and the boat began to pull away from the quayside.

44. Ingrid Steen

Ingrid was unaccustomed to having so many people around her. Riche was filled to the gunwales with dinner guests. All around her were TV celebrities, politicians and high-profile journalists, digging into their meals. The ones without tables were thronging around the bar, which was just a couple of metres away from the dining areas.

The bar at Riche was known as the shark pool – it was where the separated over-forties went on the hunt for a new life partner. Somewhere a glass shattered.

'. . . and then he said that this wasn't what he'd envisaged his life being like, that he'd dreamt of something else. You know? He's forty-five but acting like a kid. He's a man, not a fucking boy. Zero sense of responsibility.'

'That's too bad,' said Ingrid, shaking her head and lifting a piece of fish to her lips.

Carina Feldt was an old colleague from her days at *Aftonpressen* who had changed careers five years ago and become a publisher. She had spent the last six months embroiled in a toxic divorce from the father of her two children, Gustaf Hammar, the PR king of Stockholm.

One day after putting the kids to bed, he'd told her it was over. He didn't love her any more, he wanted more time for himself. There was no room for negotiation, nothing to think through – he'd already bought himself a two-bedroom flat at the other end of town.

'So now he takes the kids every other weekend – that's all he does. He's living like a twenty-year-old. Hitting the bar with his employees, getting home at dawn and embarrassing himself. It's tragic.'

'Tragic,' said Ingrid.

Ingrid felt sorry for Carina, but she was having a hard time engaging. Her thoughts kept wandering off to the MS *Ocean Star* and Tommy. Everything was in place, she had done her part, and anything that happened now was beyond her control. There was nothing she could do to help. The boat should have sailed by now with the party in full swing. Tommy was probably standing around getting fresh with Julia – probably more or less openly.

Ingrid longed for it all to be over. For the moment when Tommy was revealed to be a crackhead and his whole reputation as an honourable, serious journalist was thrown to the wolves.

Carina got up to go to the ladies', disappearing into a mass of people at the bar. Ingrid put her hand in her bag to pull out her mobile, but her fingers brushed something else instead.

45. Victoria Brunberg

Victoria needed to get closer to Tommy, to talk to him, but that young woman didn't leave his side. They were two hours into the voyage, sources of light outside the windows were becoming ever more sparse and the hacks around her were getting increasingly inebriated. Victoria was still at the bar, responding monosyllabically to any attempts at conversation while continuing to keep an eye on Tommy.

A band were getting ready to come on stage. When they picked up their instruments and a singer with a mop of blond hair and a leather jacket grabbed the microphone, there was uproar in the room. Victoria glanced across to where Tommy had most recently been standing. He was gone. She quickly began to scan her surroundings and spotted his back. The woman was nowhere to be seen; perhaps she'd gone to the loo. Instead, Tommy was talking to the man who had welcomed the guests earlier in the evening. Victoria had to act now. She had gone over what she would say several times. She took the wine glass with her, making her way through the crowds whose attention was now fully directed at the stage.

Victoria touched Tommy's elbow, leaned forward and whispered her rehearsed phrase. It was drowned out by cheers as the singer on stage grabbed the microphone and said a few words. Tommy stared at Victoria uncomprehendingly. 'I work at the Russian embassy. I have information about acts of espionage against Sweden,' said Victoria, more loudly this time. 'Follow me, we need to talk.' Tommy's jaw dropped, but he quickly pulled himself together.

He nodded, gesturing towards the back door by the bar. No one seemed to pay them any attention; everyone's eyes were glued to the stage where the singer had started her first song. They quietly walked down a deserted corridor, their footsteps echoing ominously. They stopped outside a door with a window in it, leading out onto the deck.

'Out here,' Tommy said, holding the door open for her.

Victoria noted with relief that the deck was empty. She headed towards the stern to ensure that they wouldn't be discovered even if some passenger gasping for a cigarette showed up. Tommy was a couple of steps behind her as she turned the corner and stood by the metre-high railing.

The boat was leaving foam and white ripples in its wake in the dark water, which was fringed on either side by wooded shorelines. Tommy stood beside her, leaning his elbows on the railing. She put down her handbag between them.

'You said you work at the Russian embassy?'

Victoria avoided his gaze, nodding quickly.

'My country is spying on your country – we're bugging your newspaper.'

Tommy stroked his chin. He seemed sceptical.

'Why are you telling me this?'

'Because I want to leave Russia and seek asylum in Sweden.'

Tommy got out a pack of cigarettes and waved it in Victoria's direction. She helped herself to one before he took another out for himself.

'I quit ages ago, but I'm still an occasional social smoker,' he said by way of explanation as he lit her cigarette. Their eyes met for a second in the dim glow of the flame flickering in his cupped hand.

It felt intimate – there was something attractive about him.

The cigarette didn't light.

'Let me,' she said.

She took the lighter and the cigarette from Tommy's mouth and stepped out of the wind. Tommy turned back towards the water and waited for her. One hard shove was all it would take.

'How you getting on?' he asked over his shoulder.

'Almost there,' she said.

Victoria quickly took off her high heels and hurled herself towards him.

46. Ingrid Steen

The wine was gone, their plates had been removed from the table by a waitress and the conversation was beginning to die down. The pauses were becoming longer. Carina's eyes were shiny with exhaustion and booze. The auditory accompaniment from the bar was growing louder and louder, the wall of people moving closer to Ingrid's table as the crowd grew in size. Ingrid was in high spirits – she wasn't sure whether it was the alcohol or the fact that she was noticing that men still looked at her with hungry eyes. Probably a combination of the two. Especially one man at the bar, who had awakened her curiosity. He appeared to be in his thirties, with dark brown hair, and was wearing a black shirt and black jeans. Time after time, his gaze would linger on her without any hint of embarrassment, and Ingrid stared directly into his bright eyes.

'Time to make a move, don't you think?' said Carina, reaching for her coat.

'Definitely,' said Ingrid.

At the same time, she didn't want the evening to end. She didn't want to go home to the big empty house in Bromma.

'Wait a second,' she said. 'I'm just going to the ladies.'

Ingrid sensed the man at the bar watching her as she

gathered up her things and pushed her way towards the toilets.

Once she had closed the cubicle door behind her, she got out the bag of cocaine from her handbag, found an old, wrinkled banknote and quickly laid out a line. She'd never tried drugs – apart from a few puffs of hash one weekend in Copenhagen during her youth.

She sucked up the powder, using her phone's selfie camera to make sure her nose wasn't white. Then she opened the door. The world began to spin, becoming softer and a little more electric. She quickly made her way through the venue to Carina, who was waiting by the table.

Out in the street, they embraced in front of the line of taxis.

'You can have the first one,' Ingrid said, gesturing towards a waiting Taxi Stockholm cab. She remained where she was, waving as Carina got into the back seat. Once the car had disappeared, she turned around and headed back into Riche. She immediately sought out the man in black by the bar. He looked surprised. Ingrid felt full of self-confidence.

'Do you live nearby?' she asked right away.

'In Vasastan.'

'Good,' said Ingrid. 'Give me the address. Then leave and take a cab there.'

He laughed.

'Thirty-five Odengatan.'

Five minutes later, Ingrid was in the back of a taxi driving along Birger Jarlsgatan. Her heart was pounding, her head pleasantly spinning. She discreetly put a hand between her legs and felt that she was wet.

47. Victoria Brunberg

She saw Tommy fall soundlessly through the air – it was only when he was a metre or so from the water that he screamed. His body vanished into the dark sea. Victoria stayed by the railing. A couple of seconds later, Tommy's body appeared – he was waving and screaming for all he was worth. She checked with a glance over her shoulder that no one was approaching, then she raised the lighter to the cigarette before taking a long drag.

His body would shut down before he reached the shore: he would freeze to death. He hadn't seemed like a bad man, but what did Victoria know? The woman who wanted him dead probably had her reasons – just like she had with Malte.

Victoria checked her wristwatch and realised her hand was shaking. They ought to be on the way back to Stockholm. She returned to the party. The band were still on stage, the blonde singer singing for all she was worth, leaning back with her face pointing towards the ceiling. No one had seen a thing. Victoria returned to the same spot as before and asked for a glass of white wine. She felt calm. In an hour or so the boat would dock at Nybrokajen and then she would slip away unnoticed. People were already so hammered they barely knew their own names. But what next? Where was she going to go?

Back to Russia? She thought about Al and her body felt warm. She liked him; he had treated her decently. Not like Yuri, but he was a man who understood women. A proper man. Perhaps she should accept his invitation to celebrate Christmas in Barbados. But what would she do between now and then?

48. Ingrid Steen

The man was waiting outside the main door, which was next door to a bar with smokers standing outside in clusters dragging on cigarettes. He proffered his hand to her and introduced himself.

'Lukas.'

'Charmed,' she said with a giggle. 'You can call me Johanna.'

He frowned.

'Call you?'

'Yes. It's not my real name, see. You going to open up or what?'

Lukas shrugged, tapped in the code and held the door open for her. Ingrid felt amused by the situation and by being in control. In the lift they stood opposite each other, Ingrid scrutinising him from head to foot with no embarrassment. She liked what she saw. He met her eye and smiled.

'You're good looking. Did you know?' she said.

He laughed.

'You too.'

It was a small two-bedroom flat on the fourth floor, with windows facing onto Odengatan. Ingrid didn't take off her shoes – she went straight to the window. Lukas approached her, stood close by and put his hands on her waist. Her body tingled, but she could feel the drug wearing off.

'Wait a second,' she said. 'Where's the bathroom?'

Lukas pointed her in the right direction. She took her bag with her, laid down a new line on the loo and snorted it. She felt her heart beat faster and her body temperature rise.

He was still by the window. She squeezed in between him and it, and sat down on the window ledge, drawing him to her. They kissed. He tasted of booze. She unbuttoned his trousers, taking his hard cock in her hand. His breathing got heavier and heavier.

Down on Odengatan, a drunk shouted.

She fumbled with her own clothes until she stood in front of him naked but with her high heels on. Ingrid leaned her upper body against the window and arched her back inwards.

PART 3

49. Ingrid Steen

The Swedish flag fluttering outside the building was at half-mast.

Ingrid was wearing black. Even though it was winter and the sun hadn't shown its face all week, she had concealed her face behind a pair of oversized sunglasses.

She opened the door and got out of the car. Mariana Babic had been waiting inside the sliding doors to meet her. She gave her a long, warm hug.

'Are you going to be okay doing this?' she said softly.

Ingrid nodded with gritted teeth.

Someone must have warned the staff in the newsroom that Ingrid was on her way up. The team were gathered around the central desk. Ingrid acknowledged a few familiar faces while trying to spot Julia. Tommy's office was empty, the desk groaning under flowers.

The Group CEO Ingvar Svedberg put an arm around Ingrid, leading her carefully to the middle of the room. Ingrid kept her eyes fixed straight ahead. Ingvar cleared his throat.

'Tommy Steen was one of the finest people and most courageous journalists I have ever met. *Aftonpressen* is in mourning, the Swedish media is in mourning. We've been robbed of a strong, important voice in social debate . . .'

Ingrid stopped listening, continuing to search for Julia's face among the journalists present.

When being questioned by the police, Ingrid had hesitantly admitted that Tommy used coke and that she'd tried to get him to stop.

She had also reluctantly explained that two weeks ago she'd realised that Julia Wallberg, *Aftonpressen*'s celebrated TV presenter, was the person who was helping him to get hold of the drugs. The police had exchanged glances. Ingrid knew that the Stockholm cops loved putting away people in the public eye for drugs offences to show the wider public and politicians that they took the issue seriously. Every famous person caught up in a raid was a publicity coup for the police, and Ingrid was certain they would move against Julia. Hopefully it would result in them searching the presenter's apartment, and that would see her hitherto successful career brought to an end. Everyone in the room probably already knew that the police had found a bag of cocaine in Tommy's jacket pocket and that the tox screen had shown he had coke in his system when he'd gone overboard.

The information had already got out online and on social media. Ingvar Svedberg could talk about Tommy's splendid qualities until he was hoarse, but in the eyes of the public he was nothing more than a crackhead who had gone at it and then fallen overboard at a company party.

'An accident, a terrible accident has left an incredible woman without a husband and a beautiful little girl without her beloved father . . .'

Ingrid pursed her lips. Ingvar cleared his throat, took a deep breath and collected himself.

'I'd like us to honour Tommy's memory with a minute's silence.'

50. Birgitta Nilsson

Birgitta had been keeping an eye on Lovisa all day – it was the girl's first day of school since her father had been found drowned in the archipelago. While it pained Birgitta to see the girl so silent and absent, she was in agreement with the head and the school welfare officer that it was in Lovisa's best interests to get back into her daily life as soon as possible.

The other pupils were quieter than usual. They understood, they were showing respect. Birgitta was proud – this was a wonderful class she had in her charge. One day they would grow up to be good, capable members of civic society.

Just as Birgitta emerged into the playground, she saw Lovisa with her mother heading for their car. Ingrid Steen was wearing black. Unable to stop herself, Birgitta called out her name. Ingrid turned around, said something to Lovisa and came towards Birgitta.

'I just wanted to offer my condolences,' said Birgitta. 'What a dreadful, tragic accident.'

'Thank you,' said Ingrid.

She searched for more to say.

'Lovisa, she's . . . you have a wonderful, courageous daughter. You can be proud of her.'

Ingrid Steen nodded and was about to head back to the little girl.

'You probably have lots of lovely friends looking out for you, but if you need anything then don't hesitate to get in touch,' said Birgitta.

'Thanks,' said Ingrid, before turning away.

Birgitta watched them go for a while before hurrying homewards. She needed to cook a big meal for Jacob and the twins. It was the last time they were going to see each other, and she wanted them to have a good time together. They'd sigh at her hopelessness, roll their eyes on the few occasions when she opened her mouth. The passing of the years had left her accustomed to this and mostly indifferent, but it still hurt. Sometimes she wished she'd had a daughter too. Girls were softer than boys. Life might have felt simpler if she had had someone who loved her back.

51. Ingrid Steen

The bushes and trees separating each garden from the next were leafless and bare. The temperature was heading for freezing. Ingrid had had no idea that the street was so close to her own home. She'd had to stop herself from looking for the name of the woman whose husband was going to die soon. Perhaps it was someone she knew? Someone she had bumped into in the supermarket? Someone with a child in Lovisa's class at school?

She pulled her hat further down over her ears.

The houses with their Christmas star decorations in the windows looked so peaceful. Everything indicated that the people who lived here were normal, decent sorts. Yet there was at least one woman who hated her husband so much she was willing to kill him. There were probably more.

Detached houses in suburbia were women's prisons without walls – the women were kept there through love and duty to their children. Ingrid wasn't going to murder a man – she was going to liberate a woman. Just as she had been liberated by Tommy's death.

52. Birgitta Nilsson

The house was silent. Jacob was snoring beside her. Birgitta stayed awake, even though sleep was whispering to her temptingly. Jacob sometimes used sleeping tablets – it had been no trouble grinding a few more into his nightcap.

He was going to die. She was going to keep her promise to love him and be faithful for better or worse until death parted them. Birgitta was going to be at his side until the end. He had picked her, and she had been flattered, had mistaken his reticence for goodness. The evil that you learn to identify as a child is loud. Her body still bore the marks of his evil.

Birgitta carefully pushed aside the duvet, crept downstairs and unlocked the front door. On her way back up, she couldn't help but go into Jacob's study.

The candles were on the windowsill. The silver candelabra had been inherited from Jacob's mother. Three weeks after her death, he had used it to strike Birgitta. Not her head. No, he had swung it against her side while the twins were asleep. He had broken two of her ribs. Birgitta had lain awake for weeks afterwards. Jacob had always been capable of controlling his evil acts. And Birgitta had learned to control the physical pain that Jacob's violence gave rise to. Birgitta doubted that he had ever committed an act of violence against anyone other than her. When the twins had been born, she had been afraid he would set about them. She had promised herself early on that if he raised a finger to either of them she would kill him. But he had never touched them – no matter how much they had screamed, fussed and fought.

Birgitta heard a sound from the doorway.

'What are you doing in my study?'

53. Ingrid Steen

Ingrid contemplated the two-storey house. She quickly checked her watch. It was time. The front door was supposed to be open; all she was going to do was light a candle and then she was going home. She looked around and pushed open the gate. She crept across the hard, frozen lawn. By the front door, she stopped and listened. Silence.

'Upstairs, second room on the right,' she repeated to herself.

She carefully pushed down the door handle and stepped inside. She pulled out some blue polythene overshoes from her pocket and put them on over her shoes. She could smell dinners, life, unfamiliar people. On the wall to her right were framed photographs. She ignored them. She didn't want to know – couldn't know.

Ingrid crept as far as the stairs. Took a step. Two more. Suddenly she came to a halt. She could hear noise from upstairs. A voice. A man's voice. Dogged, almost hissing. She heard a thud. Ingrid spun around, preparing to rush outside.

54. Birgitta Nilsson

Jacob pushed her against the wall.

He couldn't be awake – it was impossible. She had crushed two sleeping tablets into his whisky. Hadn't he drunk it?

Jacob righted her, took aim and hit. The air was forced out of her body as his fist struck her belly. Birgitta collapsed. He looked at her in disgust.

'Spying on me? Bloody hag. I said you could never come in my study.'

He never gave her the chance to reply. He kicked. Birgitta held up her arms. His foot struck her elbow and Jacob grimaced with pain. His eyes lit up – glowing with fury.

The woman, the one who was meant to come and light the candle and make sure that it started a fire, ought to be here any moment now. Perhaps she was already in the house? But what could she do? Obviously she'd leave. Birgitta didn't blame her.

'Please, Jacob, I—'

He bent down and grabbed her hair. Dragged her head up until it was level with his. Birgitta ended up on her knees, whimpering pathetically.

'The belt,' he hissed. 'You're going to get a taste of the belt, you fucking bitch.'

He let go of her and drew the curtains.

55. Ingrid Steen

The knives were in a row, shining amongst the washed-up crockery. She put on the thin gloves, selected a large, sharp steak knife and weighed it in her hand. She had heard enough. She crept back to the stairs and began to move up them. Faint sobs. Somewhere in the house a door opened.

'Why the hell won't this bitch do as she's told?'

Ingrid crouched at the top of the stairs. The man was heading her way – she still hadn't seen him. Ingrid felt nothing but rage as she waited. The footsteps got closer, increasing in intensity. He was coming back, towards her. When he was around a metre away, Ingrid hurled herself forward. At the last moment, he must have heard her, because he spun around, managing to raise his arm, and she felt the pain as something cut across her cheek.

But it was too late. She had already buried the knife in his stomach. He gasped, staring at her uncomprehendingly. His mouth was open – there was a gurgling sound coming out of it. She withdrew the knife and stabbed him again. And again.

He collapsed on the floor. Ingrid stopped stabbing and contemplated the lifeless body. What was she meant to do now? She had stabbed another person to death.

She heard weak groaning noises. They were from the room with the closed door.

'He's dead,' she said. 'Are you okay?'

Silence.

Ingrid repeated her question.

'I'll manage,' the woman replied.

Ingrid wanted to go in there to hug her, to comfort her, to explain that her personal hell was over.

'Stay where you are,' said Ingrid. 'We can't see each other's faces.'

She thought for a moment.

'What happened tonight was a burglary gone wrong. You both discovered the thief, and he killed your husband. I'm going to take the knife with me. I have to go now – call the police as soon as I'm gone.'

'Oh God, thank you.'

Ingrid looked around, and her eye caught sight of the belt lying a little way from the man. That must have been what had caught her on the cheek. She picked it up and stuffed it into her pocket.

EPILOGUE

Around a year later

The air was warm and even though the sun was setting the temperature in southern Florida was well over thirty degrees Celsius. Two women were sitting at a round table at a beach-side bar with ocean views. They could occasionally hear the sound of engines or car horns from the road. Ingrid Steen and Victoria Brunberg had never met before, but they shared each other's darkest secrets. Conversation between them was faltering, cautious and polite.

'You said you'd been to Barbados?' Ingrid asked.

'Yes, for New Year. I was there last year too – with my fiancé,' Victoria Brunberg replied.

'Is he kind?'

'Very kind.'

Victoria raised her drink to her lips and drained what remained in the glass.

'And you?'

Ingrid shook her head.

'No, I live alone with my daughter.'

She gestured towards the beach, where a blonde girl was playing in the waves.

They hadn't revealed their names to each other. It was safest that way. They were still waiting for a third person. She was another woman they had never met before and they didn't know what she was called, but she was also part of the way they had freed themselves.

Around them were mostly tourists. Couples were photographing each other or gazing at the turquoise sea. The women both jumped when a police cruiser drove past with its sirens blaring. Once it had disappeared they laughed uncertainly.

'Where can she be?' Ingrid Steen asked.

'Maybe she's not coming.'

'Let's wait a bit longer.'

They called the waiter over and ordered another mojito each. The server returned with them on a tray. The glasses were misted, the mint bright green under the layer of ice. An older woman appeared, looked around and then approached their table.

The chair legs scraped as she pulled it out from under the table. Her hair was white and she was rather skinny. Her face was pale and didn't quite fit in with the other sun-kissed tourists.

She stared at the older of the two women at the table. Victoria Brunberg's gaze flickered questioningly from one to the other.

'Do you know each other?'

Ingrid Steen and Birgitta Nilsson continued to contemplate each other before bursting into laughter.

TRUTH OR DARE

PART 1

1

'Walk Like an Egyptian' is on the radio. Liv Andreasson likes the song. The taxi driver, who smells of sweat and has microscopic red pimples along the hairline on his neck, is bopping to the music. Every once in a while, he glances at her in the rear-view mirror and each time she averts her eyes.

It's OK, Liv thinks to herself. I forgive you for smelling of sweat and for licking your lips when you saw me coming out of the building, even though I must be at least thirty years younger than you.

Four years ago a Taxi Stockholm driver saved her life, which is why she is loyal to the firm. Unlike her friends, she never takes an Uber.

The driver's gaze seeks out hers again.

She turns her head and takes in the city.

A dark, snowy Stockholm is flickering past outside the window.

Winter streets, winter land.

The people out there are well and truly wrapped up, with thick down jackets covering their smart clothes, while their breath rises in plumes of steam in the gleam of the streetlights.

'Walk Like an Egyptian' fades out and a breathy DJ says

that there are just over six hours of the year left. She began applying her make-up in the afternoon in the studio apartment on Valhallavägen. Liv actually lives at home with her parents. She's rented the flat secretly via an ad on Blocket. It's been hers for three months and she's got it for another three to come. The woman who owns the flat has gone to Bali to find herself. Liv spends as much time there as she can. She goes straight there from school. She lies to her parents, telling them she's sleeping over with friends. And that she's got homework to do and needs to study. After all, she is graduating from sixth form this summer.

She's never felt tempted to show off her hiding place. Well, there is one person she'd like to invite there. But she knows it'll never happen.

The taxi rounds the corner, drives through the tunnel and a moment later the expanse of the Söderström River opens before her. Across the water she sees the glitter of the city's tens of thousands of lights. The car makes a thudding sound as the tyres carry it onto the Danviksbron Bridge. Liv reaches for her handbag, gets out the vodka-filled Sprite bottle and raises it to her lips. She rummages in the bag. She finds the tablet loose in the inside pocket and pops it into her mouth. It lingers on her tongue and the familiar, bitter taste spreads through her mouth.

'You had a good day then?' the driver asks her.

'So so. My mum died two weeks ago.'

The lies come so naturally nowadays. The first time she lied about her mother was at a party around a year ago. All of a sudden, the words left her mouth and when she noticed how shocked the guy she was talking to was, the feeling was liberating. Almost intoxicating. In Liv's eyes, it was as if she didn't exist. If her mother didn't exist, then she couldn't let her down.

The man's eyes widen. Liv feels the sense of satisfaction warming her from within. He's off balance. Fumbling. Looking for the right words, trying to say something comforting, but in the end he settles for mumbling, 'I'm sorry.'

'We weren't really that close.'

The scenery is becoming increasingly familiar. It's here, in Skurusundet just outside Stockholm, that she grew up. Liv and her family moved here from Örebro when she was four. The houses are big, overlooking the narrow strait. The finest among them look directly out onto the water, naturally. If you happen to be on a boat, the panoramic windows are transformed into aquariums, inside which wealthy people live their lives. Liv knows. Her family lives in one of the aquariums. Only taxis are moving up and down the quiet street now; the SUVs and sports cars are parked on driveways or at rest in garages. Most of the houses are in darkness. The residents of Skurusundet usually celebrate New Year abroad. In Chamonix, the Seychelles, St Anton or the Maldives. Liv's Instagram is a round-the-world-trip at this time of year.

The driver pulls over and Liv hands over her card, taps in the PIN and pays in silence. She climbs out and adjusts her short dress.

A cold wind makes her shiver. Her heels are four and a half inches high and make her legs look thinner and longer. Hopefully even thinner and longer than Martina's. While they might be best friends, everything is still a competition between them. They've always competed, while at the same time providing unerring support for one another. Their relationship is anything but uncomplicated.

Her foot goes through the ice into a frozen puddle on the driveway, and she staggers and swears. Bloody typical of her. She immediately looks up towards the house to make sure that no one saw her, while grabbing hold of the handrail to steady herself as she climbs the three slippery steps. She rings the bell.

The door opens immediately.

'You're early,' says Max, who is wearing dress trousers and

a shirt, his bow tie hanging undone around his neck. It's unusual seeing him like that. He usually wears a leather jacket and T-shirt. His jeans are often tatty. Somehow he gets away with it among all the pullovers and pastel shirts worn by their classmates each and every day.

'I was just changing,' he adds, stepping to one side.

She tries to interpret his voice. Is he happy or would he have preferred to be alone for a little while longer? Max is a strange one. Sometimes she can see right through him, as if she understands every single cell in his body. Other times, he's a stranger – it can be as if they don't even speak the same language. Despite the fact they've known each other since they were kids. He runs his gaze over her short, black dress but says nothing. His expression doesn't give anything away either. All it does is take it in.

She follows him inside. At three storeys, the house is one of the biggest and most luxurious in the neighbourhood. The bottom floor is one massive open-plan space with views across the dark strait of water, and that's where they're going to see in the New Year. A kitchen area with a huge island and dining table for at least twelve dominates one half of the room, while the other half is occupied by two enormous Svenskt Tenn sofas upholstered in a classic Josef Frank fabric. It's like a large drawing room, decorated with a mixture of the priciest design classics and valuable heirlooms that doubtless made the auctioneers at Christie's pale with envy. It's clearly intended to impress visitors.

Max's dad is a senior executive at a bank; his mum is a housewife. Although in her case the word housewife is misleading. She doesn't actually look after the household. Nor did she look after the kids when they were younger and everyone still lived at home. They have servants to take care of all that. Max is the youngest of four siblings and the only one still at home.

The dining room with its large panorama window is

adorned with small explosions of glitter and gold. A banner suspended from the diamond chandelier above the table says *Happy New Year!* Set on the marble-topped kitchen island are four ice buckets with bottle necks peeking out. Although there are only four of them coming, there must be at least forty wine glasses and champagne flutes lined up.

'You've made it so pretty!' Liv says with a laugh. 'But why so many glasses?'

'So you don't have to drink out of one more than once.'

'There's going to be a lot of washing up tomorrow.'

'Not my problem,' says Max with a shrug. Liv positions herself with her back to the kitchen island. She runs her fingertips along one of her arms, her skin reacting and a shiver running through her body. At first she thinks she's cold, but then she realises that it must be the tablet beginning to have an impact.

'Let's have a shot while we wait for the others,' says Max, heading over to a glass cabinet with built-in lighting. He takes out two shot glasses, puts them down on the marble countertop beside Liv, retrieves a bottle of Absolut vodka covered in condensation from an ice bucket and fills the small glasses. He runs his finger across the stray drops and then puts it in his mouth. Grimaces. Then he repeats the movement and proffers his finger towards Liv. She licks it. Quickly. She'd rather let her lips linger, but she doesn't dare. Silently, they raise the shot glasses towards each other, tip their heads back and down the vodka.

Both splutter and put down the glasses.

'Your parents have already arrived. The oldies are partying like there's no tomorrow,' Max says.

This time Liv can't avoid hearing the contempt in his voice.

He waves Liv over to the window. He points towards the house next door. Liv immediately recognises her mother from behind, her long red hair trailing down her bare back. She's talking to Max's dad. Liv counts a total of eight people.

There, among the heads, she spots the man who took her virginity against her will four years ago. She's not seen him for a while and her body involuntarily tenses. An image flashes through her head and suddenly her body is ice-cold. She quickly glances at Max to see whether he has noticed anything, but he's still staring intently at the other house. Liv would really like to point at the man and say, 'He raped me', but she buttons her lip. She's never told anyone. And how would Max take it? Would he be disgusted by her? More than likely.

'Can you make me a cocktail?' Liv says, tugging him by the arm and steering him towards the booze.

'What do you want?'

'Surprise me.'

'What, do I look like some sweaty bartender?' Max says, stony-faced.

Then he cracks a smile. He fills two glasses with ice, pours in a lot of booze and tops them up with soda. He hands a glass to Liv. She takes it and they toast each other. They hook their right arms together at the elbow, and laugh so much that most of it ends up on the floor and their clothes.

That makes them laugh even more.

But suddenly Max stops laughing and breaks free. Liv spins around. Martina and Anton are standing there watching them. Martina's eyes are ping-ponging back and forth from Max to Liv. Flickering. Worried. But not angry. More surprised.

She's taken off her coat to reveal a sequined dress. She has black high heels on. No doubt there are several photos of her outfit up on Instagram already. Her blond hair tumbles over her shoulders and down her back like a waterfall. If she's jealous, she isn't showing it.

Anton is standing next to her. His hair is slicked back. He's wearing evening dress. His leather shoes look too big. He comes over to Liv while Max kisses Martina. As Liv allows herself to be embraced by Anton's big body with its scent of

Calvin Klein, she sees Max tilt Martina back – as if they are in some old Hollywood flick – and theatrically kiss her.

'Fuck me, we're going to have a good night,' Martina says, before dragging Liv to the bathroom. Martina hoists up the sequined dress with a total lack of embarrassment, pulls down her lace pants and sits on the toilet seat. Liv leans her back against one of the two wash basins.

Martina is her best friend; she loves her. Even though they no longer see each other after school since Liv got the apartment at Gärdet. She should probably have told Martina about it. But she wanted something that was just hers. A place where she could be alone and come down. And she isn't sure that Martina would get it. Or be able to keep quiet about it.

Martina rambles on. Liv can hear but she isn't listening. There's a knock on the door.

Max's voice.

'It's me.'

'Wait a sec,' says Martina. She stands, pulls up her knickers and straightens the dress. She inspects her face in the mirror before nodding at Liv, who unlocks the door. Liv leaves Martina and Max alone and heads back to the dining room as she hears the door close and the lock turn.

Anton is standing in the same spot where just a couple of minutes ago Max put a finger in her mouth. He has his phone in his hand and all of a sudden, the speaker system crackles. Music pounds through the room from all directions. Anton is saying something, his lips are moving, but the music – Liv thinks it's Rihanna – drowns out everything. He lowers the volume, puts the phone back in his dress trouser pocket and meets her halfway across the room.

'Jesus, you look good,' he says. 'Total fucking model.' She notices how he's trying to sound confident and relaxed, but she knows he's nervous. His throat is flushed red. He reaches for a drink.

'You too.'

She likes Anton. He's counted among the popular guys at Skuruskolan School – probably because he's Max's best friend. He lives in Max's shadow, just like Liv has lived and worked in Martina's shadow since primary school. As soon as Max and Martina come back, Anton's focus will shift to Max. He'll puff out his chest and as usual he'll joke about Liv's neckline or ask her to suck him off, then let out that braying fake laugh of his.

Liv doesn't blame him. He has to entertain Max. All the time. He has to be just a little bit worse while also putting Max on a pedestal. That's his job. His mission.

Anton is standing by the window. Liv looks at him – he's handsome but he has none of Max's radiance, that confidence that you've either got or not. Now he's staring towards his own house where the party for their parents is in full swing. A man in white is moving around serving canapés, and you can almost make out the tinkle of champagne flutes.

'Do you suppose they're having fun?' she asks.

'I was just in there, so I *know* they're not. They're projecting onto each other. Talking about their own success. Discussing their companies, cars, holidays – stuff that means nothing. Gossiping about how unhappy or how much of a failure everyone else is. You know how it is. And one day we'll be just like them. It's actually pretty tragic.'

'Do you really think that? That we'll be standing there in a few years' time, just as empty as they are?' she asks.

Anton laughs.

'I'll bet you that twenty years ago they said exactly the same things about our grandparents. To be honest, it's insane how long this friendship has been passed down the generations.'

Liv sees the man who raped her reach towards the tray proffered to him and then watches him wolf down a canapé. She thinks about his lips, his teeth, and she knows exactly what they feel like.

'What is it?' Anton asks.

He's watching her closely.

Liv comes to.

'Nothing.'

'You looked really fucking weird. Are you pissed or something?'

She nods.

'Yes, must be. I was drinking while I got ready.'

'Didn't your parents notice?'

She's on the verge of confessing about the apartment, but catches herself.

'I've got a few bottles hidden in my room.'

Anton smiles, wanders over to the sink, leaves the tap running while he gets out a glass. He waits, tests the temperature with a finger before filling it up. He's given her water before when she's had too much to drink, and he knows she likes it ice-cold. He passes it over to Liv, who gratefully accepts. She likes it when Anton is kind and considerate.

While she drinks, she thinks about Max and Martina in the loo. They're probably having sex. According to Martina, they do it a lot. Two or three times a day. Perhaps Max has his finger in Martina's mouth right now, just like he did in Liv's. Their saliva is being mixed. Via Max.

It was almost four years ago to the day that he raped her for the first time. In the boot of his BMW X6. She was on her way home from an indoor bandy match, and he pulled up alongside her and asked whether she wanted a lift. But instead of taking her home, he asked whether it was OK for him to run an errand. He turned off onto a forest track leading down to a frozen, secluded beach. Stopped the car. His hand sought her out, first brushing her shoulder, then making its way towards her breasts and then between her legs. His mouth was half-open. Suddenly he let go of her, opened the car door, walked around to the passenger side and opened her door, then

151

led her across the frozen grass to the back of the car, threw open the boot and told her to lie down. Her legs were dangling off the edge and he fumbled as he pulled off her tracksuit bottoms and knickers. She didn't protest – just lay there as if she were paralysed while he thrust into her.

Later, that same night, she put on a thick coat and sneaked out while her parents were asleep. She tried to get a grip on what had happened – whether she had actually been raped. She hadn't said no. She hadn't struck out, kicked or bitten him. She had just been totally paralysed. How could he have been so sure that she wouldn't tell anyone?

She wandered aimlessly towards town. She left the protection of her cosy suburb. She followed the long cycle trails, passing through neighbourhoods with tower blocks and shopping malls, past pretty houses from the turn of the nineteenth century. As if anaesthetised, she walked through cold and darkness. Felt nothing, thought nothing. Or rather, she thought the same thing over and over again. What exactly was it that had happened? Before she knew it, she'd been walking for two hours. She came to a stop on the Danviksbron Bridge. For a while she looked down into the darkness below, then she heaved herself up onto the railing. There was very little traffic; it was almost non-existent at that time of night. But a car stopped behind her. She heard the tyres shriek and squeal. Liv turned her head. She read 'Taxi Stockholm' on the liveried car. The driver was a woman. She was short and plump and looked like a stocky penguin.

'Don't do it!' she yelled. 'For the love of God, don't do it!'

Liv didn't reply, just turned back to face the darkness again. The woman made an effort to calm herself. When she next spoke, her voice didn't sound as shrill and desperate. She approached slowly. Crouching.

'Sweetheart, please don't jump. No matter what's happened, it'll get better. Remember that you have a family that loves you. You've got a whole life ahead of you.'

Liv looked over her shoulder. The woman was crying, the cold and wind making her cheeks red. She reached forward with her hand in a pleading gesture. To this day, Liv had no idea why she'd taken the woman's hand and climbed down.

They hugged, then the woman drove Liv home.

'Do you know when the food's coming?'

Liv is abruptly roused from her reverie and the memory of the woman who saved her life that night dissolves like a soluble tablet. Anton looks at her. Liv is suddenly conscious that she is squeezing the empty glass very hard. She puts it down.

'I think the caterers are coming at nine.'

'I'm already hungry.'

Anton rubs the palm of his hand over his tummy like a child. Liv smiles. He puts his hand in his pocket and pulls out his mobile.

'Who the hell wants to wait? I'm going to order a home delivery,' he says to himself. 'Yep, that's what I'll do. Some panting little Indian is going to have to cycle over with a pizza for me.'

Liv stops listening and wanders over to the console beneath the wall-mounted TV at the other end of the enormous room. She presses the panel to make it open. She contemplates the contents. What are they going to do for six hours? Drink, obviously. Eat. But she wants something to occupy her. On one of the shelves she finds an old edition of Monopoly. She pulls it out. She tentatively removes the lid, checks the board and cards. Without thinking about what the others will say, she goes over to the sofa, unfolds the board on the table and begins to set out the metallic gaming pieces.

2

Max is staring at the Monopoly board set up on the table. He shivers involuntarily. The evening seemed more than promising until a few moments ago, but now he quickly looks around to make sure the others haven't noticed the shift in his mood.

It was after a games night when Max was ten years old that the first signs of schism appeared. From the outside, Johan – Max's oldest brother who works for a bank in London – is still part of the family, where everything other than maintaining the facade of perfect family life comes second. But it was after that evening of Monopoly around eight years ago that Johan finally broke away from his father. After punching him. In the eye. It was as if their childhood had suddenly burst its banks within Johan.

Chaos had erupted. Afterwards, Johan had disappeared, running away from the house into the bright summer night. Max's mother fetched a bag of frozen peas, which his father held to his injured eye while he scrutinised the remainder of the family with his other eye and told them that none of them could ever speak to or of Johan again. Max, his two siblings and his mother complied and obeyed. They kept quiet.

Just like they always had.

Although Max is angry that Johan disappeared, he knows that he did it for him. That it was an attempt to protect himself and Max.

Since that day, Johan's name has not been uttered inside the house.

But what his father doesn't know is that Johan calls Max twice a year. On Max's birthday – 19 June – and every New Year.

Max wonders whether Johan will call tonight.

He hopes so, but you can never be sure.

Max places two fingers between his throat and his shirt collar and eases the pressure of the starched fabric. Martina has insisted he wear the bow tie properly, but it feels ridiculous. They're just a group of four friends who have known each other since birth, but she wants everything to look perfect on her social media. It won't be long before she drags him out onto the terrace overlooking the water to force him to pose with her for a selfie.

'Four,' she calls out, picking up her piece – a racing car.

She moves the piece and ends up on the dark blue square for Norrmalmstorg.

'I'm buying it.'

Anton grabs his mobile phone from where it's lying on the table and looks at it in irritation.

'Stupid fucking Indian. He's got lost. How bloody hard can it be to deliver a Hawaiian? No wonder your job's cycling around with fast food, you pathetic ape,' he says to the screen.

No one reacts. They're used to Anton's outbursts.

'Look,' Anton exclaims. He holds up the phone to show them the display. 'Now he's stopped, probably having a look around, doesn't give a fuck that the pizza will be cold when it gets here. They've got no work ethic, those Foodora couriers. I should send an email to his bosses to say they should fire him. We'll say he groped Liv. I guess the problem is that no one would believe she didn't want him to. The whole neighbourhood knows she's easy.'

He laughs and seeks out Max's gaze.

Max smiles fleetingly, leans back on the sofa and yawns.

Liv waves her arm towards Anton as if to slap him, but he lunges out of the way. When she sits down again her dress has ridden up her thigh and Max can see her black panties. After a while, he forces himself to avert his gaze.

'This is boring as shit. We need to up the stakes,' he says.

The hubbub from the others falls silent immediately, as if someone has switched them off.

'What did you have in mind?' Liv asks.

'Paper money is worthless,' says Max. He puts down his drink, picks up a fistful of banknotes, holds out his arm and lets them flutter onto the carpet. 'We're not kids, right? This is what we're going to do: we're going to invent our own rules. When you land on a street owned by someone else you can either pay . . .'

'Or what?' Anton asks expectantly.

'Or choose to play truth or dare.'

Martina nods, as does Liv.

'Look at Liv,' says Anton with a smirk. 'The mere thought of intimacy has her panting. Probably best we put a plastic bag on the carpet or it'll be ruined.'

Martina laughs while Liv pretends not to have heard what Anton said. Something tells Max that she is upset by Anton's constant digs. But what should Max do about it? Surely it's up to her to tell him herself that she doesn't like it? After all, they've just agreed they're not kids any longer.

It's Martina's turn and she rolls the dice. She moves her token to the yellow zone: Vasagatan. It's owned by Anton.

'Truth,' she says.

Anton leans back while sipping his drink and looking at her.

'How many people have you slept with?'

156

Martina rolls her eyes and glances anxiously towards Max.

'I don't care,' he says.

He means it. He really doesn't care. He's only slept with three people, even though he usually tells people he's been with around fifty girls.

'But I don't want to say.'

'Come on, you're a good girl,' says Anton, knocking back what's left of his drink. The ice cubes clatter in the glass. 'I bet it's not more than five.'

'Seven.'

Max takes the dice. Shakes. Releases. They roll across the table. Stop. A four and a three. Max picks up his iron, moving it seven streets along, ending in the pink zone: Odengatan. Martina turns towards him.

'Are you going to pay?'

Max considers it. He contemplates the bundles of cash on the carpet. He shakes his head.

'Forget it. Truth.'

'Which of your siblings do you like best?'

He frowns. 'What do you mean?'

'You and your three siblings are in a room together. A guy comes in with a gun. He asks you which two he can shoot. Which sibling will you save?'

Liv and Anton are looking at him expectantly.

'What a fucking sick question.'

Without being able to stop it, Max watches the memory being replayed in his mind's eye like a film, watching as Johan's right fist strikes his father's eye. His father falling, shouting, flailing to the floor. Johan towering over him, raising his fist again, but stopping. Clearing his throat. The gob of spit hitting his father on the cheek.

Don't touch him again. Get it?

Max is staring dead ahead.

'Johan,' he says quietly. The only one who has ever protected him.

He gets up, wanders over to the kitchen island and fetches one of the ice buckets. He sets it down on the coffee table.

One by one, they fill their glasses.

The doorbell rings.

'Finally,' Anton exclaims, getting to his feet. 'Come to the door with me, Max.'

Max does as he's told. He opens the door and outside on the step is an older man in a pink quilted jacket with a hat underneath his bike helmet. The man passes a pizza box over to Anton.

'Enjoy,' says the delivery guy in accented English, smiling and turning away.

Anton opens the lid and puts a hand on the crust of the pizza.

'Wait,' Anton says.

The man stops and comes back.

'It's cold,' Anton says in English, with an affected Indian accent. 'The pizza is fucking cold. Did you stop to eat curry or what?'

The man holds out his arms.

'I'm sorry, sir. I fell off the bike. The streets are icy this time of year.'

'Moron. You should go back to Bombay.'

The man grits his teeth and stares down at his feet. Max feels sorry for him – why does Anton always have to be so harsh? At the same time, he gets it. Who wants to eat a cold pizza?

Anton regards the man in irritation.

'Maybe you could heat it up if you have a microwave?' the delivery guy says in a conciliatory tone.

'If we have a microwave?' Anton says with a laugh. 'Yes, we have a microwave. But your job is to deliver the pizza warm.'

'I'm sorry. I really am.'

'You know what? You should pay for this. Otherwise I'll

make a complaint to your bosses. I'll tell them that you were rude. And that you took a bite of my pizza. My friend Max here will back me up. What about that? You'll lose your so-called job.'

'Please, sir. That's not fair.'

'The world isn't fair.'

Max can see the man nodding slowly and getting out his mobile phone. His hand shaking, he taps in Anton's number. The sound of the notification announcing the arrival of funds buzzes from Anton's mobile. As if it were about money. Anton hands over the pizza box to Max and checks the amount. Snorts. Then shuts the door in the man's face.

'Fucking cheek of that guy,' says Anton as Max hands back the box.

While Anton goes to microwave the pizza, Max crosses to the window that overlooks the house next door. At the other party, his father is laughing while talking to Martina's mum. He makes a sweeping gesture with his arm and guffaws. The perfect family man. Max can feel the fury creeping in – just like on so many occasions before.

Liv has crept up beside him without him noticing. They stand there in silence, shoulders brushing against each other.

Last summer they kissed. At least that's what Max thinks – that's how he remembers it. They were drunk at some house party a few houses down the street. They'd probably smoked some weed too. Martina had faceplanted on one of the sofas. The birds were singing, the night was bright and warm and they decided to head down to the water for a swim. They stripped to their underwear and jumped in. Next thing he knew, they were kissing each other. Liv tasted of liquorice and tequila. Waist-deep in the water, she clung on to him. He realised she had nothing on her bottom half – he could feel her sex against his thigh.

'Never tell Martina about this,' she whispered before

159

swimming back to the jetty, drying off, quickly dressing and heading back to the house.

They never mentioned it again. But Max has thought about it. Many times. He wants to ask Liv about that night. Did they really kiss? Or was it just a fantasy? He's not sure – he was so drunk. And high.

'Does it upset you when Anton says . . . stuff like that?' he whispers instead.

Liv turns her head and looks at him in surprise, as if she wonders whether he means it. Then she shakes her head.

'No, why would it? He doesn't mean anything by it. You know what he's like.'

They return to the sofa. Anton has cut the pizza into slices that he distributes. He pretends to drop the pizza and delivers a quip that makes Martina laugh loudly. Even Liv smiles.

It seems to Max that the jargon between them is often harsh, but there's a unity that can't be put into words. The rest of their year are at a big party, but Max, Anton, Liv and Martina prefer to meet up here. They like it best that way. Even when they're surrounded by other people, it's always just the four of them. Ever since kindergarten and even before that. Dinners, holidays, riding school and golf lessons – all together. They've gradually grown up together, just like their parents. But perhaps especially in the last few years – it's as if they've built a wall to keep out the outside world.

He pulls Martina towards him and presses his tongue into her mouth; she responds to his kiss even more greedily. She tastes of oregano. Pineapple. Tomato. Max swallows her saliva, aware that Liv is watching them. He has a guilty conscience. Towards whom he isn't sure. He lets go of Martina.

'Whose go is it?' he asks, looking around.

'Mine,' Liv replies. She grabs the dice and throws them. Two fives. She bounces her ship along the street. It ends up on orange: Karlavägen – Max's street.

'Dare,' she says.

'Make out with Anton,' says Max.

'For real?'

Anton sits up, looking expectant.

'Or you can go outside and roll around in the snow.'

'Sure. If you fire up the sauna.'

Anton slumps again.

'It's already on,' he replies.

Liv smiles at Max.

Then she gets up slowly, heads for the hallway, pulls her dress over her head and covers her breasts with her hands. Max takes note of the black knickers and that she isn't wearing a bra. The memory from last summer flickers by again. The others put on their coats and shoes and head outside. Liv throws herself into the snow with a scream, rolls around, leaps up and jumps up and down on the spot.

'Jesus-fucking-Christ-it's-cold. Jesus-fucking-Christ.'

She bounces up and down. Howls. Races past them, down the stairs towards the basement where the sauna is. Max can hear her bare feet pattering on the floor and then the sound of the sauna door being yanked open.

Max, Martina and Anton return to the living room.

'Whose go is it?' Anton asks.

'Liv's. Again. She rolled two fives.'

Anton picks up a slice of pizza, folds it and inserts it into his mouth.

'When's the caterer getting here?' he asks while chewing.

'I told them to serve the food at nine, so they should be here at eight to start laying the table and getting things ready.'

'What are we having?' Martina asks.

'You'll see,' says Max.

'Exciting,' she says flatly. 'Let's get on and take that photo now. Here.'

She passes her mobile to Anton.

Martina checks that her dress is right, fiddles with Max's bow tie and holds up his dinner jacket. He slides his arms into it, runs a hand through his hair. They open the door to the terrace. Max shivers and flicks the switch. Suddenly they're bathed in the glare of the strong floodlights. They raise their champagne flutes, leaning against the balustrade. Max puts an arm around Martina's shoulders. She positions one leg in front of the other – it makes the legs look thinner, she once told him – and then she smiles.

'Try to look a bit happier, Max, old boy,' says Anton.

He snaps a few pictures, Martina changing position while the smile remains permanently affixed to her face.

'Show me.'

The smile fades away and Martina frees herself from Max and goes over to Anton to grab the phone back. She examines the photos carefully.

'Good. You've nailed it,' she says appreciatively.

'I've had to learn. I think I must have taken over ten thousand photos of you two!' Anton says.

Liv is watching them through the window, she's put her dress back on, her hair is damp. Her face is red with the warmth. Or the cold.

Max turns off the lights on the terrace and they go back inside. Martina announces that she needs a couple of minutes to pick a photo and then edit it. She has 11,000 followers on her Instagram account and twice that on Snapchat.

Anton pours a drink. And then downs it.

'Time for a slash,' he says. He burps and disappears to the loo.

Max and Liv sit in silence. She is sitting on the floor with her legs crossed, barefoot. He's on the sofa. Legs parted. He recalls something Anton told him a while ago – that he'd seen Liv going into a block of flats around Gärdet.

They concluded she was most likely sleeping with some older guy there.

'Are you seeing anyone?' he asks while pouring champagne into her glass.

'No.'

'Anton says you've got a guy in town.'

Liv frowns.

'He's talking shit.'

'He says he saw you going into a block of flats on Valhallavägen a couple of weeks ago. With a guy who was, like, forty.'

'He's not right in the head. A stalker – that's what he is.'

Liv takes a few sips of the champagne. Then she sets down the glass.

'But no,' says Liv, suddenly looking Max right in the eye. 'I'm not seeing anyone. I haven't been for a long time.'

The others come back, sit down and they resume the game. Now and then, Max gets out his phone to check it. Johan hasn't called.

Just as it's Max's go, his mobile begins to vibrate. He immediately recognises Johan's number. He takes the phone out onto the terrace. He slides the doors shut before answering.

'Hi, bro!' says Johan. 'How are things?'

'Good. How are you?' Max asks.

'Oh, you know. Good. About to sit down at the table. How are you celebrating this year?'

'Round at ours.'

'Alone?'

'No. Anton, Martina and Liv are here.'

'Where are Mum and the others then?' Johan asked.

'Truls is in Skåne. Sara's in Åre. Mum is at Anton's. They're having some kind of party.'

Johan laughs. A cold gust of wind blows in off the water.

'But you're good?' Johan asks. His voice is tender. Possibly worried.

'Jesus Christ, yes. Top notch.'

A brief silence follows.

'I'm going to be a dad,' says Johan. 'It's a girl; she's due in June. Might be the same day as you.'

'Congratulations. What are you going to call her?'

'Don't know yet. Any suggestions?'

'No. But I'll give it some thought.'

'Good. You do that. I haven't told anyone else. It's still early days. But, well, now you know. You could come over to see her in the autumn? You'll have finished school by then.'

'That'd be fun,' says Max.

'Definitely. And we can go and watch a match together. Arsenal. Or maybe Chelsea? On me.'

A woman's voice on the other side of the North Sea says something to Johan. He replies in English.

'We're going to eat now. But it was good to talk. Be in touch with you about that trip. Take care of yourself, little bro.'

Max hangs up, squeezing the mobile in his hand as he leans on the balustrade. He stares into the darkness. He replays the conversation word-for-word. He's pleased for Johan. His throat feels tight. A tear runs down his cheek.

He takes a deep, cold breath.

Someone is knocking on the glass behind him. He quickly wipes away the tear before turning around.

Martina holds out her arms on the other side of the window.

'Who was it?' she asks when he slides open the door to step back into the warmth.

'Caterers,' says Max. 'Said they were struggling to find the place.'

3

Martina Liska doesn't really like alcohol, yet in the short course of this evening she has already knocked back two glasses of champagne and two shots. She's a lightweight really. She'd prefer not to drink at all, but she knows she wouldn't be able to cope with the pressure and questions from the others. If there's one thing that Martina really hates it's when other people ask her things – that makes her feel abnormal and like an outsider.

The room spins occasionally. She sneaks a glance at Max as he moves his piece across the board and hears him say 'dare' when he lands on someone else's street.

All the time, she is positioned so that she can see what is happening in the other house. She doesn't really need to be able to see her mother to know what is going to happen. She's still careful in her movements. Martina knows that they become more sweeping, her voice higher pitched, that she'll probably end up aggressive or sentimental or teary.

'Shave off your hair,' says Liv.

Martina comes to. Did she hear that right? Liv and Max are looking at each other and then he begins to laugh.

'Rubbish. He's not going to shave off his hair,' says Martina. She looks sternly at Max.

'You really can't shave off your hair. I won't allow it.'

Liv attempts to interrupt and say something. Defend Max. Possibly get Martina to see the funny side. But why would it be funny to wander around looking like a freak?

Martina leans forward and holds up her hand towards Liv. 'Excuse me, I'm actually talking to my boyfriend.'

Liv falls silent immediately. But just as Martina is about to explain to Max, he gets up. Martina's jaw drops. She feels humiliated. With Liv and Anton on his tail, he heads for the bathroom. She is about to follow when she sees her father standing talking to the woman that he's sleeping with. In the background she catches a glimpse of her mother, Victoria. She doesn't seem to be taking any notice of them. Perhaps she's already too drunk? Martina forces herself to follow the others.

Max is sitting on the toilet seat with a towel wrapped around his shoulders. Liv is clutching an angrily snarling set of clippers that she runs through his hair. A few dark clumps are already lying at his feet.

'Let's go for a Mohican, Liv! Just shave him on the sides,' Anton calls out.

Martina wants to scream. She wants to rush over to Liv and yank the clippers out of her hand, but it's too late. The others are laughing loudly at what's happening. Martina feels like crying, while also being ashamed. What does it matter the type of haircut Max has? Really? It doesn't matter at all, but she has noticed he doesn't listen to her any more. Her views, which he used to hold in such high regard, mean nothing to him now. And she's terrified of that. Because she knows that's the beginning of the end.

When Martina and Max first got together, Martina was incredibly happy. It felt so right – like finally finding her way home. They were good together – it felt like everyone at school was jealous of their relationship. When exactly did it start to go awry?

Martina can't bear to watch. She turns her back to the others, their exhilarated voices ringing in her ears, and returns to the living room. She grabs a bottle of vodka from the ice bucket on the kitchen island.

She unscrews the cap.

She tilts her head and takes a few long swigs. The booze tears at her throat and warms her belly. She stifles the impulse to gag.

She needs to relax. She's pissed off with the way she's behaving.

'Stop it. Take it easy. Be amazing and he'll like you more, you'll see,' she whispers to herself.

Where does the need for control stem from? She knows she shouldn't behave the way she does with Max, and that her demands can be unreasonable. Verging on neurotic. Yet she can't help it. But Martina knows why she behaves this way. She read a post by a psychologist on an online forum – that she would rather die than admit to having visited – which said the children of alcoholics often develop a strong need to control their surroundings because they've felt powerless since childhood.

Martina sinks heavily onto the sofa. She stares into space.

The first time she realised that her dad, Karl, was unfaithful was three years ago. Her mother was already drinking then. And Martina hated her for it. But that was when the secret drinking which had previously been inexplicable – at least for Martina – became explicable.

Somehow it became easier to cope with.

Martina discovered it when they were on a family holiday in Thailand. She borrowed his mobile on the sly to check out the photos he'd taken of her that day and see whether there were any she could use on her social media. When a notification for an incoming text message appeared, she opened it on a reflex and saw that it was from Nicole. It was obvious they were in a relationship. There were even nudes of her in the thread. But what hurt most was the message in which he said how bored he was on the trip. And how much he missed her and wished he'd gone away with her instead. After reading the conversation, she'd been unsure whether her mother knew about the infidelity. Martina clicked through to her parents' messages and realised right away that her mother was fully aware of what was going on.

Rancorous texts from her mother about how humiliated she felt.

Furious outbursts about what an awful person he was.

Sometimes she threatened to tell their daughters.

Martina checked the times the messages were sent. Not infrequently the messages were sent during dinners on their trip, when the four members of the family were spending time together.

Martina had had no clue.

It was as if she was living with two strangers. Who had apparently lost all love and respect for each other.

For the rest of the holiday, she didn't exchange a single word with her father. He kept asking whether she was angry with him, but she didn't reply.

The toughest thing is that Martina can't talk to anyone about it. Not to her mum, who she pities – she is clearly a complete wreck. And not to her dad; he would never understand – after all, he is the one who has driven the entire family into the abyss. And not to her best friends. What would they think? She knows that if this came out in her group of friends or at school then it would not only affect her but also her little sister, Adrienne. And she wants to protect her at any price. Little Adrienne: she is still so innocent and defenceless. Although she is almost ten years younger than Martina, they are close. Martina doesn't want her little sister to be betrayed by grown-ups in the way that she was. She is going to make certain of it.

Of course Martina knows there are cracks and secrets in

every family. Once Max let slip that he'd been beaten by his dad as a child. But the following day, when Martina asked him about it, he got angry. He said she must have misunderstood what he'd said and urged her to drink less.

The sound of her friends' cries and laughter grows louder and eventually they emerge. Max looks ridiculous. Liv has pretty much shaved his head bare. Only in the middle is there an uneven stripe of brown hair. Martina forces herself to laugh too. She notices that Max relaxes and looks happy. He puts an arm around her. Her body feels warm.

'I'll take the rest off tomorrow,' he whispers to her.

There's something conciliatory about his voice.

'You can wear it however you want,' she whispers back. 'I still think you're the handsomest guy in the world.'

Liv is about to roll the dice when the doorbell rings.

'Catering,' Max says, getting up to open the door. 'Let's go upstairs while they set up.'

Martina pulls out her phone and takes a photo of the game before she and Liv pick up the pieces and carry them upstairs. They say nothing to each other. There's something else that Martina has begun to notice more and more: she and Liv work best in the boys' company. They make an effort. Joke. Have fun. When they're alone they can end up a bit stiff. They've grown apart. Martina misses what it was like when they were younger. Simpler. Now it mostly feels like Liv is avoiding her, as if she's hiding something.

The room upstairs also has huge windows overlooking the water, but the view into the parental party is worse. Thank goodness.

The floor is covered with a carpet Max says cost 350,000 kronor. It's hard to walk across it in high heels and Liv slips off her shoes before they look at the photo and begin to replace the pieces on the Monopoly board.

Martina considers whether to do the same as Liv and take off her heels, but she doesn't like her legs without heels. They end up fatter and shorter, and tonight she really wants Max to think she looks beautiful.

Once the boys come upstairs, they start playing again. It's Anton's go. Two threes.

'Dare,' he says, and Martina can see him winking at Max.

She realises they've hatched a plan. And that it's to do with Liv. But when Max opens his mouth, he's interrupted by Liv.

'We left the champagne downstairs,' she says. 'I'll go and get it.'

'No,' says Max firmly. 'Anton, your task is to go down to my dad's wine cellar and fetch two bottles. Expensive ones. No fox piss. They can't be worth less than ten thousand kronor.'

'But—' Anton protests.

'I'm not done yet,' says Max. 'You'll have to google them if you're not sure about the prices. Bring them back here and I'll explain what you should do.'

Anton gets up. He lumbers off. He's clearly disappointed not to get to snog Liv. While they wait for Anton, Liv takes the vodka bottle from the table and passes it around. Martina takes a big gulp while Liv tells Max about some video game she likes. He listens with interest and Martina feels a pang of envy. Liv can make Max laugh, and perhaps above all listen, in a way that she has never managed. Especially not lately. Martina doesn't know what to do.

She interrupts, wanting to join the conversation, but notices that it dies out straight away. Instead, they sit in silence until Anton returns.

'Which one is most expensive?' Max asks.

'This one,' Anton replies, holding up the right-hand bottle.

'Pour it out.'

Martina looks at Anton, who looks uncertain.

'Pour it out?'

'Yes. On the carpet.'

170

'But your old man'll go nuts at me. What if he finds out it was me?'

Max gets up.

'We'll move the sofa, empty the wine and then put it back. No one will notice.'

Anton still looks dubious, and Martina fully sympathises. Max goes downstairs to fetch a corkscrew. When he returns, he grabs the bottles and opens them. He encourages Martina and Liv to help him by grabbing the back of the sofa and tipping it backwards.

'Right, pour that shit out,' says Max peremptorily, taking a swig from the other bottle. Anton nods, goes over to the sofa and pours the wine onto the carpet. Suddenly he stops. Instead of merely emptying out its contents he bends forward and draws a penis in red wine.

Max laughs.

'Good!'

Anton continues with renewed confidence, boosted by Max's praise. The wine is quickly absorbed by the thick carpet.

Martina and Liv let go of the sofa and it falls down with a soft thud. Nothing is visible. That's how easy it is to conceal a sin.

'Whose go is it now?' Martina asks.

'Me again.'

Anton picks up the dice. Rolls them. A one and a two. He moves his piece three places. That street is also owned by Max and there's even a hotel on it.

Max and Anton's eyes meet in mutual understanding. Now is when Max tells him to make out with Liv, Martina thinks to herself. But that isn't what happens. Max points down to the storey below where the caterers are setting up the food.

'You said you thought that piece of ass down there was fit, right?'

'Yeah.'

Max pauses. Stringing it out.

171

'Go downstairs and tell her you need to speak to her in private. And then ask her how much for a blow job.'

Martina expects protests from Anton, but instead he roars with laughter. Of course.

'Fuck, you're sick,' he says appreciatively.

Martina wants to tell them that it's not OK and that they're crossing a line. She tries to catch Liv's eye. But Liv is staring down at the carpet. Martina opens her mouth but then swallows her words. The others will think she is boring. And she doesn't want to be the one to ruin a good mood. Anton disappears downstairs and Martina stands at the window and looks towards the other house. Standing down there, next to one of the stilts below Anton's parents' house, her dad Karl is smoking a cigar.

Beside him is Nicole.

Anton's mum.

Martina sees her father quickly look around before pulling Nicole towards him and kissing her. Martina gasps and is filled with panic when she spots Liv from the corner of her eye, approaching the window.

4

The stairs creak under Anton's feet. He moves slowly, full of distaste for what he's going to do. But he knows that pulling out is off the cards. The three people upstairs are the only people he really cares about and that he knows love him. And is it so bad? The woman down there has probably been made indecent offers before. By old blokes. Fat, ugly blokes with bellies and haemorrhoids. In comparison to them, he's a real catch. Who knows? Maybe she'll be pleased and eager to earn some extra cash. He can hear the sound of clinking crockery and them chatting in a foreign language as they get things ready and set up. Anton comes to a halt on the last step in front of a photo of the Ludwigsson family.

The four children and their parents are lined up on a beach in front of a sunset, all of them in swimwear.

Anton immediately focuses on Max. He's so thin, his ribs prominent and his skin taut. His brother has an arm around him. They're looking into the camera with serious expressions. In the photo, Max can't be more than five years old. Even then, he and Anton were best friends. Anton thinks he remembers that the Ludwigssons went to Majorca.

Anton approaches the photograph, thinking to himself that

173

there's something about it that's off – something that he can't quite put his finger on.

He hears footsteps and someone stops in front of him. It's the girl that he's meant to ask the price of a blow job. She gives him a friendly smile and he nods at her.

'We're almost done. Are you hungry?' she asks.

'I'm just going to the loo,' he says, pushing past her.

Anton locks the door. He closes the toilet seat then sits down and leans forward, his elbows resting on his thighs. He takes a few deep breaths. He really doesn't want to do this, but he knows he must. What kind of person would he be otherwise? The food smells delicious. The girl's smile is imprinted on his retinas. She's sweet, seems nice. It can't be much fun having to work on New Year's Eve. No doubt she'd prefer to be at home with her friends. Where does she live? Probably in one of the ghettos where coloured people live. Rinkeby, Tensta, Hjulsta or Akalla. The blue line on the metro is often referred to as the Orient Express. Maybe she has a crook for a boyfriend and he'll try to hurt Anton when he finds out what he said?

Should he go back upstairs and tell the others he succeeded in his mission? They'll hardly come downstairs to check with her . . . He could make something up. Could say that she took it all as a joke and began to laugh. No, they'd be able to tell he was lying straight away. He's usually a good liar, but not in front of them. They see right through him. As if he were an aquarium and his emotions were the brightly coloured fish inside. It's always been that way.

He ends up thinking about the delivery guy he was so mean to. Fuck, that was unnecessary, he thinks to himself. Falling off a bike in the icy conditions could happen to anyone.

Anton gets out his mobile and transfers the money – including a big tip – back to the guy. In the reference he writes *Happy New Year*.

He gets up and opens the door with clammy hands.

He steps out. The smell of the tasty dishes in the dining room grows stronger. On one of the platters he can see big red lobsters. Slices of fillet of beef. Salads. Sauces. Far too much food for four people, obviously. There are three girls warming up the food and laying the table. Somehow it feels easier that there are no other men there.

Anton straightens his back.

He puffs out his chest and goes up to the girl.

'Yes?' she says kindly.

'I'd like a word with you,' he says sternly.

'Is something the matter?' she asks. The smile is still there, but it's strained.

The other two have stopped what they're doing.

'Could you come with me?'

You could hear a pin drop – the girl looks uncertainly at her colleagues, shrugs and follows him into the hallway. Anton has his mobile in his hand and discreetly starts the voice recorder app.

He stops by the stairs under the photo of the Ludwigsson family. He clears his throat. She's a head shorter than him, and she's looking up at him with kind, friendly eyes.

'How much for a blow job?'

For a second it looks like she's going to slap him silly.

'Sorry, what did you say?' she asks.

'A blow job. I'd like you to suck me off.'

She looks sad. Degraded. She opens her mouth to say something but Anton never finds out what her reply was going to be. She loses her will to speak. She turns on her heel and returns to the others with rapid footsteps. He stops the recording. He stares vacantly at her receding back. Mission accomplished.

When Anton returns upstairs, the mood has changed. He was so sure they'd be exhilarated and tense with anticipation, but when he plays the audio file back they don't react. Something has happened. Anton isn't sure what. He tries to read their faces but doesn't succeed.

He takes a few big gulps of wine and then puts the bottle back on the table.

'She looked pretty damn tempted,' he says, laughing. 'But who wouldn't be?'

Not even Max smiles. Instead there's just silence.

'Has something happened?' he asks.

'No,' says Liv, shaking her head.

'Are they going to be ready soon? I'm actually getting really hungry,' says Martina.

Max is semi-reclined on the sofa with a bottle of wine tucked under his arm. In the time that Anton has been gone he's fetched a new one. He looks incredibly bored, despite Anton's successful venture.

'We need to raise the stakes again,' says Max.

At that moment, Anton realises what he found so odd about the photograph earlier.

Max is talking, but for once Anton isn't listening to him.

Until they were fifteen or sixteen, Anton never saw Max in just his swimming trunks. He almost never did PE at school and when he did he'd skive the lesson after to go home for a shower. He said he found the school showers disgusting. He never went swimming – no matter how hot it was, he always stayed on the jetty or the beach.

Anton hears the sound of the dice hitting the table. He comes to. He lets go of the memory. Martina leans over and moves her piece.

She groans when she lands on GO TO JAIL.

'Make out with Anton,' says Max.

This was apparently what Max meant by raising the stakes. Martina looks at him as if she's misheard.

'With Anton? How do you mean?'

'Make. Out. With. Anton.'

Max's voice is annoyed, as if he's speaking to a stubborn child.

'But . . .' Martina begins to say before falling silent when Max rolls his eyes.

Anton is unsure. Martina is his best friend's girlfriend, his best friend who wants them to kiss. His body feels weird and wrong, although he is excited at the same time. Obviously he wants to snog Martina. Doesn't everyone?

'Please, Martina. Don't be so frigid and dull,' says Max. 'You want to, right? Anton? It's no biggie.'

Anton examines his hands and shrugs. He tries not to show that he's nervous.

Martina wrenches the wine bottle from Max, tips her head back and takes a big swig. Then she approaches Anton, who is sitting in the armchair. She straddles him. She leans forward and presses her tongue into his mouth. His head spins. Anton can feel his penis filling with blood with her this close; he can feel her saliva – it tastes of booze.

'Touch her,' says Max. 'Touch her boobs.'

Anton hesitates. Then he moves the palms of his hands from where they have been around her waist to her breasts. He rests them there. His excitement reaches new heights. Martina pushes her tongue deeper into his mouth, moving it around more and more quickly – it's as if she wants to prove that she likes it. Maybe she wants to make Max jealous? Anton responds to the kiss even more eagerly. Suddenly the tongue disappears leaving behind a void. Martina twists her face away, moves backwards, adjusts her dress and returns to her seat.

He wonders how long they kissed for.

It might have been ten seconds, it might have been ten minutes.

Anton glances at Liv, wanting to see her reaction. But her face is expressionless. Empty. There is no one who is as difficult to read as Liv. Despite his having spent so many hours, so many years trying to do so.

He knows about the apartment she has in Gärdet. When he brought it up with Max he was forced to add the thing about her being with an older man to provide an explanation for why he followed her. To make it seem more natural. He's wondered why she hasn't told any of the others about it – it's weird, inexplicable, but he doesn't want to betray her. Something inside her is broken – there's a piece missing, and he spends almost every waking moment wishing he could mend her. Deep down, he knows that it's Max she's interested in. It's impossible to avoid seeing how jealous she can be sometimes. But until last summer, he was certain that Max was completely uninterested.

Anton stood by the window, saw them go into the water, swim and splash and laugh. Be natural in a way he had never been able to achieve with either Liv or any other girl. It was as if they were two completely different people than the ones he knew when they were alone.

And then, as if in slow motion, he saw Max lean forward and kiss her. He saw how she eagerly returned it before swimming away.

Just like now, with Martina, it was impossible to tell how long the kiss lasted.

He's convinced that Martina knows nothing about Liv and Max.

Perhaps, Anton thinks to himself, this is Max's way of making up for his guilty conscience. Now it's one-one.

While Anton has been lost in his own thoughts, the game has moved on. It's Liv's go. Anton misses what her dare is, but sees her disappear downstairs with Max trailing behind her.

Anton and Martina stay where they are without looking at each other.

Silent.

Embarrassed.

He takes the bottle of wine, raises it towards her and says 'cheers'. She replies joylessly with Max's wine bottle. Anton considers whether she is disgusted by him – maybe he has bad breath. The next moment, he wonders whether Max and Liv are kissing downstairs. And for the first time in his life, he wants to tell Martina what he witnessed on that warm summer's night. Max knows, just like everyone else, that Anton is in love with Liv. Even so, he has to have her too. Even though he has Martina.

When he looks up, he sees Martina wiping away a tear from her cheek. It's left a white stripe in her make-up.

'What is it?' he asks.

'Nothing,' she says.

For a second, he thinks she knows too. He wishes it was true.

'Your mum . . .' she says before falling silent when she hears someone coming up the stairs.

Max is standing there.

'They've gone now – it's time to eat. Pack up the game and bring it downstairs – we can carry on after dinner.'

He turns around and disappears.

'What were you going to say?' Anton asks after a while.

'Nothing.'

'But—'

'Nothing. Didn't you hear what I said?'

Martina stares at him angrily. Anton stands up on trembling legs and staggers over to the window. He looks towards his own house. There are a couple of shadows smoking by the stilts that hold up the house.

Behind his back, Martina has begun gathering up the game pieces after photographing them again. It's too risky to stand close to the stilts like their parents are doing. He wonders whether his dad has told the others that the wood is starting to get brittle, but they can't afford to deal with it right now. His father has, in confidence and while hammered on expensive whisky, explained to Anton that his estate agency is in a tight spot. They're on the verge of bankruptcy. Made him promise not to tell anyone. Least of all Anton's mum. Instead of feeling sympathy for his father, all Anton feels is contempt and disgust.

His father has always gone on about how smart and talented he is – how he's the best real estate guy in Sweden. That he could sell snow to an eskimo. But now? He can't even afford to fix his own house – they may not even be able to afford to stay in Skuru for the summer. If things don't improve soon, they'll have to move to a flat.

Anton would rather die than tell anyone. Even his best friends.

PART 2

5

The food is amazing. There are many things that Liv cannot bring herself to enjoy, but food is not among them. She's glad about that. She's not Martina – who after each meal offers a smiling apology, vanishes off to the loo and sticks her fingers down her throat. Early on, Liv tried talking to her best friend about it, but over time she has accepted that this is how Martina deals with things.

She can only hope that one day her friend will stop suffocating herself from within.

Max, who is sitting at the long side of the table and has a white cloth napkin tucked into his collar, raises his glass.

'Here's to you, my best friends, and to the fantastic year we're going to have.'

The others raise their glasses in return. The meal is consumed in silence. Liv glances towards Martina, who is prodding the lobster with her fork. She skewers a tiny, tiny piece of white flesh. Raises it to her mouth. And then chews with a vacant stare.

Liv can tell she is thinking about what they witnessed from the window a little earlier. About her own reaction to it. Not because it happened but because Liv saw it too. Martina is always so anxious about what others think about her and her family – the exterior is important to her. That's why it's such a heavy burden.

But Liv already knew that Martina's dad sleeps around.

When spending her evenings in town, Liv usually frequents a Chinese restaurant near Karlaplan. She goes there to drink and draw in her sketchbook. Sometimes she reads novels that no one remembers any more. They're always written by angry young women.

One of those evenings, she was at her usual table close to the bar, giving her a full view of the premises. Karl came in accompanied by a woman who was only a few years older than Martina and Liv. They drank and laughed together. When the waiter asked whether they wanted to order food they merely waved him away. After an hour or so they disappeared, entwined and laughing, into the November night.

When Martina and Liv were standing side by side at the window a little earlier and saw Karl kiss Anton's mum, it was Liv who broke the silence.

'Pig,' she said simply.

At first, Martina looked like she wanted to protest, but her mouth remained shut. She didn't even ask Liv to keep the secret – she knows how good Liv is at keeping things to herself. There's no secret so great that it cannot be contained within Liv's slender body.

Liv suddenly feels angry – she squeezes the wine glass so hard that the top of it shatters. Startled, the others look up from their plates, taking in the blood dripping from her hand onto the white tablecloth.

It's just a scratch; she can barely feel it.

'What happened?' Anton asks in surprise.

But Liv can't bring herself to reply. Max grabs the napkin from his collar and hurries over, applying it to Liv's injured hand and pulling her with him towards the bathroom. Anton and Martina watch them go, wide-eyed.

He turns on the light, pushes Liv down onto the toilet seat, and opens a cabinet.

'Does it hurt?' he asks anxiously while rooting around.

'Not really.'

After a while, the wound stops bleeding, though the napkin is stained with patches of red. He drips some kind of stinging spirit onto her hand and examines the wound with a grave expression before sticking a big plaster over it. Liv feels so ridiculous, although she is happy to be alone with him and pleased by the worry and tenderness he is exhibiting.

When he is done, he sits down on the bathroom floor with his back resting against the wall. They look at each other but say nothing. Max reaches forward with his hand and places it on Liv's bare knee. His hand is still. The touch is electric. She both wants and doesn't want it to wander up her thigh.

But nothing happens.

Eventually, Max gets up and unlocks the door.

When Liv and Max return, they try to resume the meal but the modicum of party atmosphere that was at the table before seems to have been vanquished in its entirety. After a while, Anton suggests they carry on drinking and go back to the game instead.

They get up from the table, leaving the plates, glasses and heaps of leftovers where they are. Martina excuses herself and heads for the toilet. Liv glances at Max to try to suss whether he gets what is going on, but he is untroubled, talking to Anton while they set out the game.

Liv goes over to the window and takes in the party in the neighbouring house. The man who raped her is talking to Karl, Martina's dad. She wonders what they're talking about. They seem to be having a nice time, like two completely normal men swapping stories, and it occurs to Liv that this is exactly what they are: normal men. Overwhelmed with sadness, she checks that the others aren't watching, then takes

185

a white tablet from her handbag, pops it into her mouth and swallows.

'Are you playing with us or what, Liv?'

Martina inserts a piece of gum into her mouth, hugs Max from behind with her hands around his chest and kisses him on the cheek.

'I'm coming,' says Liv, sitting down in her spot.

When Liv rolls the dice and ends up on Valhallavägen, where Anton has just put up a hotel, she says 'truth'. She doesn't feel like doing some childish dare. Anton is clearly disappointed. He reaches for his glass while thinking.

'Who took your virginity?' he asks.

The others stare at her expectantly. She's previously told Martina that it was a guy on a family holiday to France. What has she told Max? She can't remember. She desperately tries to get her pack of lies in order. Her head feels cloudy. In her memory, the car is swaying in time with the man's thrusts, her sex is stinging and the boot smells rancid thanks to some rotting banana in a gym bag somewhere.

'Out with it!' says Anton excitedly. He leans back and laughs. 'Or was it a three-way? Two guys fucking you while you were suspended between them like a spit roast?'

Liv can feel her eyes stinging; a tear runs down her cheek. Perhaps it's the booze, or perhaps it's the tablets. Maybe it's that there are so many secrets and lies that they're overflowing. She doesn't know. All she knows is that she's crying and can't stop the tears from coming out. The others stare at her in horror.

'Fucking idiot,' Martina yells at Anton.

She hurries over, crouches at Liv's side and puts her arms around her waist.

'What is it? Liv, my love, what is it?'

Liv waves her away, hastily drying her tears. She manages to pull herself together.

'Nothing. I think I must be drunk.'

'Do you want to re-do your make-up?'

Liv smiles inside. Martina's biggest concern is that Liv might feel ugly. She could hate her for it, but instead she pats her on the hand and shakes her head.

'It's OK.'

Once she's pulled herself together, they pretend nothing has happened. As if it was just a passing rain shower that has been replaced by sunshine.

'I'll do a dare,' Liv says, taking a few gulps of booze. No one dares to protest, even if it's against the rules.

The tablet is working more quickly than the first one; the room is spinning. It feels as if she can hear her heart pounding down in her ribcage. Du-dunk. Du-dunk.

'Anyone got a suggestion?' Anton asks cautiously while looking around.

Max is staring expressionlessly at Liv.

'Take one of my dad's golf clubs, go over to Anton's and smash one of the headlights on one of the cars on the drive.'

'Surely there are cameras?' Martina says, horrified.

'No, they don't work any more,' Anton interjects.

Liv gets up without saying a word. She finds the bag of golf clubs in the hallway, picks one at random and heads out. It's cold. The wind is groping her body as she creeps towards the boundary between the two houses.

She stops behind a leafless bush, surveying the parked cars. There's the SUV she was raped in. She leans her head back and can hear the sound of laughter and music from the upstairs window. Can see the silhouettes of people.

She turns around and spots the faces of her three friends pressed to the window inside Max's house.

Liv raises the golf club, but then lowers it. She takes off her high heels and puts them slightly to one side. She grasps the club again, raises it and wallops the rear window, which shatters with a crash.

She jumps backwards.

She stands there for a second as if she's paralysed, taking in the gaping hole before picking up her shoes and rushing towards the street so as not to leave any prints in the snow.

She expects someone to turn off the music, to hear shouting voices, to be chased . . . but nothing happens.

Max opens the front door for her and she throws herself back into the warmth, panting.

She feels joyously alive.

She passes the golf club to Max, who returns it to the bag.

'Did they notice anything?' she asks, between breaths.

'Nothing,' says Anton. 'The music was probably too loud. Or they're just too hammered.'

They sit back down again. Martina fetches a towel, which she wraps around Liv's ice-cold feet. Anton shakes the dice and is about to roll them when he stops mid-movement.

He looks at Liv questioningly while putting his hands in his lap.

'By the way, why did you smash up your dad's car?' he asks.

6

The call with his brother is still echoing around Max's consciousness. Part of him wants to ask the others to go home and leave him in peace with his thoughts. He feels torn. On the one hand he's pleased for Johan. But there's also a gnawing anxiety. Johan has always said that Max is the most important person in his life. That's going to change – soon there will be another person that Johan loves more and devotes all his care to.

'Max?'

He jumps as his thoughts are interrupted. He looks up. The other three are staring at him in amusement.

'You own Norrmalmstorg. You've got to decide what Martina should do,' says Liv.

He nods absent-mindedly.

He thinks Liv is beautiful. If he asked them to leave, he'd prefer it if she stayed. He loves talking to her. She gets him, in a way that Martina never has and never will.

To buy a little time, he takes a sip from his glass even though he's heavily intoxicated. He can barely taste it, he has no idea what he's drinking, only that it's alcohol and that it loosens him up.

He has an idea.

'You've always said you think my mum is a good dresser, right?'

Martina looks at him blankly. For a second it occurs to him that both she and Anton are strangers – that Liv's the only one he really knows.

'Get a pair of scissors and cut up the five items of clothing you think are best looking.'

Martina sits up; she seems agitated.

'Wh—'

'Because this is a fucking game and you're going to do as I tell you,' he says in the aggressive tone that he knows so well and detests so much. The one inherited from his father, that he's sworn he will not allow to resurface in him. Nevertheless, he is aware that it is there within him. Sometimes it can't be stopped. Like now, when he has reacted without thinking.

Martina immediately falls silent, gets up, goes around the kitchen island and opens one of the drawers. As they hear her footsteps disappearing upstairs, Liv and Anton look down. Anton drinks his wine in a frenzy, draining the glass. He refills it.

Max is pissed off with him because he made Liv cry. Somewhere deep down, Max has realised lately that something is wrong when it comes to Liv. He can't put his finger on what. He wishes he had the courage to ask her, but he feels instinctively that she wouldn't like it. Perhaps it would create a distance between them. Liv is the most private person he has met. Her entire being is veiled in an invisible membrane, but Max knows exactly when she steps out of it.

Like a little earlier when he tended to her hand in the bathroom – that was the real Liv in there. Fragile. Vulnerable. Now she's someone else: a robot with Liv's likeness.

'What you said before, that was pretty fucking unnecessary,' Max says in a low voice. He and Anton stare at each other, unable to look away. Then Max raises his voice. 'You should stop talking to Liv like that. It's childish.'

Liv interrupts.

'It's OK, Max. I'm sure he didn't mean anything by it.'

He scrutinises her in surprise. He thought she would be happy about him defending her. Perhaps he's misjudged her – maybe she's as thick as the other two.

'OK, Anton, do whatever the fuck you like. Call her a whore as much as you want.'

Max leaps up, sending his chair crashing to the floor.

At first, he's on his way upstairs to his room, but then he realises that Martina is up there. Instead, he heads for the basement. He goes into the sauna, which is still on, and sits down on the top bench. He leans forward and lets his head hang between his knees. Beads of sweat drip onto the wood. He unbuttons the dress shirt to his belly, fumbles in irritation with the bow tie and lobs it towards the heating unit.

He buries his face in his hands.

Johan sacrificed his relationship and his position as his father's favourite to defend Max. Johan was the only one who could stand up to his father's abuse. Who struck back. So hard, so furiously, that he knocked out the tyrant. In front of the rest of the family. The one who moved to London. To freedom. Max has always dreamt of living close to Johan, getting any old job just so he could get away from his father. It has been his and Johan's plan for years. But now? Is there space for Max in Johan's life? Even when Max was alone, feeling rejected by the rest of the family, he always knew that Johan was waiting for him. Sure, his father has beaten them all. Methodically, cold-heartedly and with no apology. But Max and Johan were always the most exposed. And since Johan's betrayal, Max gets extra beatings. To this day. He is ashamed that he has never once hit back. He wishes he had Johan's courage.

'Are you OK?'

No one can move as noiselessly as Liv. No one can open a door so mournfully.

Max opens his mouth to reply, to lie and claim that everything is fine, crack a joke. But he's all out of steam.

'It's nice and warm in here, isn't it,' she says, creeping up close beside him. He can feel the sweat that has penetrated through the fabric smearing her bare arm. She puts her arm around him, gently but resolutely pulls his head down into her lap and strokes the unevenly cut hair with a maternal hand.

'My little Mohican,' she says with a sad smile. Max lets out a sob and buries his nose in the black dress.

They sit there for a while before he turns his face upward so that he is squinting at her chin and throat. He dries the tears – not because he is ashamed but because he has finished crying.

'What are you doing after graduation?' he asks.

His voice is hoarse, as if the warm air has dried it out.

She shrugs her shoulders quickly, but Max notices that the movement is a practised one and that there is an answer behind it.

'No, you do know.'

'Yes, I do.'

'Why don't we go to London? You and me.'

'Just you and me?' Liv asks, and there is a note of suspicion in her voice, like an animal sensing a trap.

'Yes.'

'It's always been the four of us,' she says, gesturing towards the ceiling.

'Always,' Max repeats. 'But I can't remember why any more.'

'Because we were the most broken ones. Functional and perfectly whole and clean on the outside, but sad and ruined in here.'

She points to her heart, which Max thinks is rather unlike her.

'But we never talk about it, not even to each other.'

Liv nods thoughtfully.

'No, but we know. And what we don't know we have a sense of. Like the fact that Anton's family are broke, or Martina's mum drinks. Or . . .'

'. . . that my dad beats me and my siblings,' Max adds. 'But I've never understood why you're broken, even though I know that you are.'

Liv's mouth forms a line. They look at each other. He doesn't want to press her.

'What do you want to do after you finish sixth form?'

'I want to get away, but I don't know where to.'

'And I can't come with you?'

She shakes her head apologetically.

'I want to travel alone. Although you're my friend, you remind me too much of . . . all this.'

Max settles for that answer. He gets what she means.

'I've got a flat in town that I rent in secret,' she blurts. 'That's where Anton saw me. There's no guy.'

'What do you do when you're there?'

'Get some peace and quiet. I draw, read books, watch TV. Sometimes in the evening I go to some bar and hang out there so that I can be alone in company.'

They hear a door open and realise that someone is on the way down to them. Max straightens up and moves a little away from Liv. The next moment, they catch sight of Martina's silhouette on the other side of the window. She opens the door and looks at them suspiciously.

'What are you doing?'

'Talking,' says Max.

'About what?'

Her gaze bounces between them.

'All sorts.'

Martina pulls out her phone and shows them the display. She scrolls from photo to photo of Max's mum's clothes, cut to shreds. It occurs to Max that the dares, the game, the whole evening in fact, feels childish. Meaningless. On the way back up the stairs, he regrets not asking Liv about the kiss last summer. Asking her what it meant, whether it really happened or whether it was the product of booze and drugs. In a way, he wishes it hadn't happened. Then he wouldn't need to have a guilty conscience vis-à-vis Martina. But if it was real, then it opens new doors in his relationship with Liv. He can't figure out what he feels about her or what she feels about him. But he knows that he can talk to her about things that he doesn't dare talk to anyone else about. Show her emotions and sides of himself that he would never dream of showing to anyone else.

Anton is slumped in one of the armchairs in the dining room. His eyes are cloudy and swimming with booze. He looks at Max anxiously.

'Come on,' says Max, dragging his friend out onto the terrace.

Anton stumbles along behind. Max knows he should apologise, set things right after his outburst. Not because he regrets it but because he knows how much of Anton's well-being is derived from him, Max. They lean on the balustrade; Anton avoids looking at him and Max is reminded of a dog who's eaten his master's food and been caught red-handed.

'Sorry if I got worked up,' he says.

'No worries.'

'But don't talk to Liv like that. It's unnecessary. I don't think she likes it.'

Something flashes inside Anton. His face shines with defiance.

'Do you think Martina likes it when you sneak off and snog all the time?'

Max stares quizzically at his friend.

'We haven't snogged.'

'Well, maybe not tonight.'

Their eyes meet. Anton looks peculiar – the aggression is directed straight at Max in a way it's never been before.

'Last summer. The party at Gustav Nyman's. I saw you in the water. Fuck you,' Anton says, spitting dangerously close to Max's feet.

Part of Max is filled with relief. Anton's words have confirmed what happened.

'You know I like her. I've told you. You got together with Martina. The fucking princess of Skuru. But you had to have them both. How the fuck can you do this to me?'

For a second, Max thinks Anton is going to punch him. But instead, his face contorts into a grimace, he lets out a sob and turns away. Max feels perplexed. He puts a hand on Anton's shoulder.

'Fuck,' Anton sobs. 'Fuck.'

'Sorry,' Max says.

They're interrupted by the sound of voices from Anton's house. It's their fathers, smoking cigars by the stilts.

Drunken voices shout towards the terrace.

'How're you doing?'

'Are there loads of chicks?'

'Don't drink the whole wine cellar tonight, lads.'

'Use a condom. I'm too young to be a grandfather.'

Laughter. Max and Anton wave. They respond jokingly to the cries. To Max, their voices sound hollow. Empty. False. Pathetic.

They call out goodbye and sink down with their backs against the balustrade so that they're not visible from Anton's house.

'I could kill him,' Max hisses.

'I hate mine,' Anton adds. 'It's awful, but that's how it is. I can't bear the thought of one day turning into him. He fucking lies about everything.'

'They're all at it.'

'What do you mean?'

195

'They lie. Pretend that everything is fucking fine all the time. But nothing's fine.'

'My dad's broke,' says Anton, exhaling. 'Fuck it, he can't even afford to repair the stilts holding up the house.'

7

Martina is in turmoil. This is the third time Max and Liv have sneaked off alone tonight. She looks at her best friend, sitting curled up on the sofa. Liv has got hotter in the last few years. She used to be nothing more than a sweet girl, but now there's something grown-up and dangerous about her that Martina envies. Something broken, but also exciting.

It's been impossible for Martina to avoid noticing how the boys' focus has been increasingly directed away from her to Liv. It never used to be like that. Martina was always the one at the heart of it all. The bull's eye. The one everyone wanted to talk to and interact with at parties.

Liv was shy and retiring.

She was Martina's plus one in every setting.

What happened? When did the shift take place? And why can't she bring herself to share the limelight with her best friend?

'What were you and Max talking about?' she asks, sitting down next to Liv.

Martina is surprised at how cold and harsh her voice sounds.

'Nothing much. He got a bit worked up while you were upstairs.'

'Worked up? Why?'

'Anton cracked one of his jokes and Max told him to quit it.'

'And?' Martina asks, annoyed that Max always leaps in to defend Liv.

'Then I said it was OK and he got pissed off with the two of us and stormed off. So I went after him to calm him down. That was all.'

That was all, Martina thinks to herself in irritation. Everything is so straightforward between them. Natural and simple. She folds her arms.

'Childish of Max to squabble with Anton. We know what he's like.'

'Yes, we do,' Liv mutters.

Silence descends on the room like a blanket and the boys return from the terrace. Both Liv and Martina get up and head back to the game. The atmosphere is tense, expectant. Not even Anton, who is usually the one to liven things up with his jokes and banter, feels up to making an effort. They play on listlessly, barely speaking.

'Shots?' Liv asks.

Mumbles of assent.

Max gets up, fetches the vodka bottle and sets down the small glasses in front of each one of them with a small click. Fills them. Martina glances at the time on her mobile: 21:37. Only a little over two hours of the old year to go.

They clink glasses, tilt back their heads and say 'cheers' in unison.

The atmosphere picks up a bit. Conversation slowly resumes.

'Music!' someone cries out.

Max turns on the music and they sway in time to it. Anton raises his arm and dances while sitting down. Liv smiles. Martina loves them – they're her three best friends and right now everything is great.

She grabs hold of Max, swirls her tongue around in his

mouth and is happy when she feels him eagerly responding to her kiss. He and Liv can talk however much they want, but it's only me he kisses like this, she thinks to herself contentedly.

'Are we ever going to get around to playing?' Anton bellows.

Martina and Max break off reluctantly and return to their seats. Martina can feel her entire body vibrating and tingling.

'My go, right?' she asks, looking around. She reaches for the dice and rolls them. She searches the board for her piece, the racing car, which is currently on Västerlånggatan, and moves it.

'You never answered the question,' Max says thoughtfully.

'Which question?' Martina asks.

'Not you,' he says, shaking his head. 'Liv.'

Everyone's eyes turn to Liv, who looks confused. Avicii's 'Waiting for Love' is booming out of the speakers.

'Why did you trash *your* car?' Anton asks.

Liv shrugs and looks down at the table. Martina and Max quickly exchange glances. It's obvious Liv is hiding something.

'You absolutely chose it on purpose,' Anton says.

'Not really – it was closest to the house. Best escape route. It might just as well have been your dad's car,' Liv says.

Martina is thinking. She maps out the driveway that she passed by just a couple of hours earlier. Since she knows that her parents arrived last at Anton's, it sounds unlikely that Liv's dad's SUV was furthest out.

'Truth or dare?' Liv asks, pointing at Martina's piece. Liv owns Västerlånggatan. There is a red hotel on the square. Martina looks at Liv.

'But seriously, Liv. Why did you choose your car?'

'What does it matter?'

Liv's voice is desperate.

It reminds Martina of her mum when she is drunk. Those trembling minutes before she bursts into tears and locks herself in her room to cry. The sobbing that cuts through the walls. Martina thinks about her father's stony face as he listens, before turning up the volume on the radio so he doesn't have to hear it. Doesn't have to take responsibility.

'It doesn't. We were just curious,' Martina says hesitantly.

But Liv's face doesn't relax. They've touched something inside her that has made her entire body issue a battle cry.

'You're all thick,' she says. 'Pathetic fucking idiots.'

She stares at them wildly.

'Most of all, you, Martina. With your boozed up alkie of a mother and an old man who can't keep his dick in his pants. You're always going on about how great everything is, how happy you are, about your fucking Instagram followers that you're feeding a completely distorted and contrived picture of your life. I sometimes wonder whether you even believe in it yourself. Your life isn't all roses and gold and glitter. Fuck me, you really should get some help.'

This is when Martina starts to lose patience. She half stands up from her seat. She wants to smack Liv. Who does she think she is? But then she sees that Liv is crying. Tears are pouring down her cheeks. Her face isn't moving, but the tears are glistening and falling and running into each other.

'My dad raped me the first time when I was fifteen. In that fucking car. In the boot. That's why I picked it. There. Now you know.'

No one speaks. The only sound is Avicii singing joyfully about leaving this world behind.

8

It's as if Liv's words have bewitched them, Anton thinks to himself.

The first one to break the silence is Max. He says that his dad beats the whole family systematically. That he has never dared to show his body because of the bruises. He talks about his brother, Johan, and how their dad drove him away after he stopped him from beating Max to a pulp.

Martina tells them about how much her mum drinks and how mean she is to Martina and her little sister Adrienne when she's drunk. She says that she still blames her dad, who has driven her to it with his constant infidelity, but that she also detests her mother for her weakness. That she is worried about ending up the same – that in some sick way it will be passed down the generations.

Secrets and lies are unravelled, brought into the light. It's like something cracking open. Sometimes the one telling their story cries, sometimes it's the listeners who cry. They refill their glasses and carry on telling their tales.

Anton thinks everything has changed and that nothing will ever go back to the way it was before. In a good way. He's never loved the other three more deeply or felt closer to them. The others have more powerful, darker stories than he does.

What does he have to be angry about?

Nothing, really. Apart from the fact that his dad is a hypocrite who pretends to be rich when he's actually up to his eyeballs in debt. And that the penny hasn't dropped with his mum. That they'll most likely be forced to move. That his dad has never been there for Anton, not in the good times or the bad parts of his son's life. Always absent. Never there with a word of encouragement or comfort. Given the context, it seems petty not to know what it is like to feel safe. But the others listen, nodding, humming along in agreement. The more he reveals about himself, the closer he gets to them. Anton has always believed it was the other way around.

'Your mum is sleeping with my dad,' says Martina. 'They're having an affair.'

'I've seen them together,' Liv adds.

And Anton nods. Tries to make out whether he is sad, but all he feels is empty and flat.

Eventually, it's as if the stories are running out of steam.

There's nothing left to tell.

They refill their glasses, then they stand in a row by the window. They silently gaze into the darkness towards the other party. Anton imagines that the grown-ups have taken off their expensive clothes and are now naked. He knows things about them that they would never ever admit – they'd rather die.

'What do we do now?' Max asks in a hollow voice.

Anton looks at the stilts under the neighbouring house. The fragile stilts that his dad has been warned about. A surveyor warned that the house was at risk of collapsing if they weren't reinforced. A thought begins to take shape in his head, growing into a roar. He glances at the others, but he doesn't dare formulate what he is thinking out loud.

At least not yet.

That would be crossing a line.

He feels Liv's hand on his arm. She is softly running it up and down as if to comfort him.

Anton is surprised and happy. He's always loved Liv.

At the same time, he feels hatred – blind, dark hatred, as he watches her dad standing and talking to Max's mum. He feels ashamed when he thinks how his words and jokes must have wounded Liv. How much it must have hurt.

'Sorry for the things I've said,' he whispers.

'You couldn't have known.'

'No, but still.'

Across the water, someone is holding a fireworks display. A rocket rises into the dark sky and explodes in greens and reds. Liv presses herself closer to Anton, puts her arms around his waist, stands on tiptoe and tentatively kisses him. From the corner of his eye, he can see Max and Martina watching what is happening with looks of surprise.

Liv takes a step back and licks her lips. He blinks at her in astonishment.

'Why did you do that?' he asks.

'I don't know,' she replies with a shy smile.

The explosions bringing colour to the dark sky intensify as midnight approaches.

The fireworks cascade down like colourful confetti above Skurusundet and Stockholm.

The group are sitting at the table.

Someone has turned down the music. They're drinking, maintaining a vicelike grip on their glasses. The game is still on the table. It's been a while since anyone moved their piece or rolled the dice.

The doorbell rings, the sound reverberating through the house. They look at each other in surprise.

PART 3

9

Voices are audible in the hall. Liv is about to follow Max to find out what's happening, when two men in evening dress appear. It's Liv's dad Markus and Max's dad Olof. They look serious, as if they're the bearers of bad news. They stagger into the middle of the room.

'Turn off the music,' Markus commands. Max does as he's told and stays by the sound system.

The two men are heavily intoxicated. They stare at the group, the Monopoly board and the empty bottles.

'Has something happened?' Anton asks.

'Someone's broken into the car,' Markus says in a hard voice, looking at Liv.

Olof, Max's dad, nods and adds:

'We thought we'd ask whether you'd seen anything?'

Their voices are slurred, their cheeks flushed with booze.

The group shake their heads. They do their best to look innocent and unknowing.

'What did they take?' Max asks.

'They didn't manage to get anything. But they've broken the back window of my BMW,' says Markus. 'Fuck, I'm pissed off about it.'

'Probably some coloured kids from Fisksätra,' says Olof.

'Seizing their chance on a night when decent folk want to relax and take some time off. Parasites.'

He makes a gesture of resignation and runs a hand through his blond hair. Liv thinks to herself that he looks like an older version of Max. They're uncannily similar.

'Have you checked the CCTV?' Martina asks.

'It doesn't work,' Anton says quickly.

'What about the police? Have you reported it?'

'We've called but they've got their hands full. Well . . . there's not much to be done,' says Olof.

'You kids have had quite a few, I can see,' says Markus, grinning and pointing to the empty bottles. He looks at Liv, who feels a shudder run through her body. But it feels different, less scary, now that her three friends know what her father has put her through.

There is silence.

'Don't let the girls go out on their own if there's a bunch of hoodlums from the suburbs running around the streets. Those bastards love raping Swedish girls,' Markus says. His words are directed to Max and Anton, who both immediately nod in agreement.

'No no, there's no need to worry. We'll look after them,' says Anton.

'No one's going out on their own,' says Max. 'We were going to stay here anyway.'

'That's good,' says Markus.

Olof and Markus nod, turn around and head out the front door. Liv hears it close behind them.

'Fucking arses,' Max mutters after a while.

Liv says nothing. Her hands are shaking. She feels sick. She finds her bag under the chair, hides a pill in her hand and pops it into her mouth when no one is looking.

'How are you feeling?' Anton asks anxiously. His voice is soft, protective.

'I'm OK,' Liv says.

'I could have killed him when he said that about rapes,' Max says.

'Me too,' says Martina.

She gets up from her seat, goes over to Liv and puts her arms around her from behind. She rocks their bodies gently back and forth.

Liv looks at Anton, who grimly raises a glass of amber whisky to his mouth.

'Would you really?' she asks.

The others look at her questioningly.

'Do what?' Max asks.

'Kill him?'

The atmosphere changes and becomes uncomfortable. Martina stops rocking them and straightens up, returning to her spot and sinking into it.

'I would,' Anton says. His lips are pursed into a single line. His eyes are dark and resolute.

Liv realises he means it. There's something about his tone, about his entire being that convinces her.

'I even know how I'd do it,' Anton adds. He shapes his lips into a smile and a hollow, joyless laugh escapes from it.

'How?' Liv whispers.

'Doesn't matter,' says Max. 'We're just pissed – of course we're not gonna kill anyone. What the hell's wrong with you?'

He looks from one to the other with a troubled expression. Liv can see him looking for confirmation, agreement, but for once no one pays any heed to Max. Neither Martina nor Anton meet his gaze.

'How?' Martina repeats.

Anton fills his lungs with air and leans back on his chair.

'The stilts supporting our house are fragile. They might collapse at any moment, and that'll take the whole terrace and first floor with it. They need repairing, but my dad can't afford to. He's been putting it off for months.'

'But if the whole house collapsed, then everything would

go, wouldn't it? Everyone would die,' says Liv. 'Not just my dad.'

Anton nods.

'Yes, everyone would die.'

He takes a sip of whisky and then raises the glass towards his house.

'Isn't that what we want? Everyone to die . . .?' he asks.

He gets up and walks slowly over to the window. He stares vacantly towards the party going on. Liv stands next to him. She can see her father in there. He's come back and is standing talking to Liv's mum. He is gesticulating angrily, probably talking about the car.

What hurts Liv most is that her mother knows about the rapes but is turning a blind eye to them. It's been more and more obvious as time passes. How can you betray your own child like that? Liv doesn't understand – will never understand. That's why the flat is so important to her, and that's why she sometimes lies about her mother. Because she might as well be dead. Liv puts her hand in Anton's and he squeezes it softly.

'Would you dare do it?' she whispers.

'I'd do anything for you,' he says.

10

There is an hour of the year left and Max thinks to himself that more has happened in the last few hours than in the preceding twelve months. How many times has he fantasised about killing his father for what he's done to the family?

Anton is right.

It can be done.

And no one would suspect them.

Especially not since their parents called the police about the smashed car window.

He looks at Liv and Anton, who are standing in front of the window staring at the house. They're holding hands and he's filled with jealousy. Something has happened – there's been a change in the dynamic between them. When? He doesn't know. But it's impossible to ignore. Max clenches his fist under the table. He thinks about his brother, all the beatings, the longing.

He gets up from the table and approaches Liv and Anton, his gaze fixed on their entwined hands. They already look like they've made up their minds.

'We're doing it,' he says. 'I want them to die too.'

The stilts are set right onto the rocks and support the entire building. If the stilts go, then Anton's house will collapse. It will be dashed on the rocks and plunge into the ice-cold water. There's no chance that anyone will survive.

'When do we do it?' Anton asks.

Max considers that a good sign. He's once again in command – the one calling the shots. He glances at his wrist-watch.

'On the stroke of midnight,' he says.

Martina squeezes in between him and the window.

'But we need to think how we're going to do this. We can never be found out – if we are, our lives will be over.'

'The quad bike,' says Anton.

'What about it?' Max asks.

'My quad bike is in the garage. If you help me to hook up a couple of chains to it, and we then attach them to two of the stilts, I'll do the rest.'

'Will two stilts be enough?'

'If it's the right stilts, then the others will snap like match-sticks because of the weight of the house. That's what the guy who came round said – that's why it was so important to get it repaired.'

Max thinks for a while.

'Will you have time to get away before the house collapses?'

'We'll have to find a long chain. Maybe even join two together.'

'What if someone goes outside for a smoke?'

'Martina and I will go over there and make sure they don't.' Liv's voice is barely audible. She clears her throat. 'I'll keep my mobile in my hand and call one of you when we go inside. That way you'll hear if anyone decides to go out.'

Max silently assesses the proposal and realises it can work.

'Right, we'll do that,' he says. 'And we'll wait until we know you've left the house. Then it's go time.'

'But we need to tidy up in here,' Martina says. 'The police are going to come here. So it'll be best if they find four suit-ably drunk youths who've had a quiet night playing Monopoly.'

11

While the fireworks illuminating the dark winter's night have intensified, Max, Anton, Martina and Liv have quickly tidied up around the house. Anton and Max have run down to the recycling point to get rid of the empties, while Martina and Liv have filled the dishwasher, leaving nothing but the Monopoly board on the table.

Martina was worried that their plans would be forgotten as their blood alcohol level came down. But it's the other way around: they are working with more focus the closer to midnight it gets.

The only thing she is concerned about is Adrienne. Luckily, she was allowed to stay at home with a babysitter tonight. When this is over, Martina is going to take care of her. Then it'll just be the two of them. Forever.

The front door opens and she hears Max call out:

'Are you nearly ready?'

Martina and Liv look at each other, glance quickly around and then say they're ready to go. All of them jostle in the hall while Martina and Liv stand in front of the mirror, smoothing out their dresses with serious expressions, checking their hair and make-up. Martina glances at Liv and wonders what is going through her head. It's impossible to interpret what is taking place in her brain. Martina is nervous even though she is firmly resolved to go through with what they agreed. She can't cope any longer. Her mother's alcoholism and meanness have worn her down over so many years. Her father's infidelity has humiliated the whole family. Martina has never felt loved. Or at least, not for a long time.

'Wait, I just need a wee,' says Liv, pulling Martina with her into the guest WC.

Martina locks the door behind them and Liv pulls down her pants and sits.

She knows Liv; she knows her friend has something she wants to tell her. Something that can't wait. Martina's heart is pounding.

'What is it?'

Liv seems worried about whatever it is she wants to say. She pulls up her underwear, straightens her back and flushes.

'It was nothing,' she says.

Martina can tell that Liv is lying. There was something. Martina is convinced that it was something she wanted to spit out before they went over to their parents. Martina reluctantly opens the door and steps out.

The boys are waiting outside, stamping their feet.

'Let's go then,' says Max, stepping outside onto the front step.

The air is cold. The smell of gunpowder lingers in the air. They walk in a line towards Anton's house. Martina hugs herself to keep out the cold. Goosebumps form on her skin. A loud firework goes off a couple of houses over. A few seconds later it explodes in the sky.

A couple of metres from Anton's front door they come to a halt. The rear window of the SUV is smashed and for a moment Martina pictures Liv with the golf club. Then the picture is erased. Instead she can see Liv with her legs parted, lying in the boot being raped by her dad. Martina notices

Anton and Max also looking at the car. Probably thinking the same as she is, she reflects.

'Does everyone know what they have to do?' Max asks.

'Yes,' says Martina. 'Quit nagging.'

She taps the mobile phone clutched in her hand, pulls up Max's number and presses *call*. Max's phone lights up and starts to vibrate. He looks at it in surprise for a moment before answering, and then inserting his wireless buds in his ears. Then he nods and he and Anton vanish off towards the garage.

Liv and Martina stay where they are, taking a few moments to prepare themselves.

Just as Liv is about to head towards the door, Martina stops her.

'Wait.'

Liv stops.

Martina takes a couple of steps forward and puts her arms around her. They embrace tightly before Martina shivers and lets go. They climb the steps. The bass from the loud music inside is making the front door shake. There are voices audible from the other side. Laughter. Clinking glasses.

Liv glances at her mobile and puts her thumb on the alarm clock.

Martina checks her wristwatch. It's a Rolex given to her by her parents for her fifteenth birthday. Well, actually, they said she could go to the NK department store and pick whichever watch she wanted – they weren't able to come with her. Twenty minutes until midnight.

The door flies open and Anton's mum stumbles, managing to stay upright thanks to her grip on the door handle.

'Why hello!' she exclaims cheerfully.

'We just wanted to pop in to say Happy New Year,' says Martina, giving her best, most dazzling smile.

'How lovely. But where are the boys?' she asks, glancing behind Martina and Liv.

Martina opens her mouth to reply, but Liv beats her to it.

'They're coming after the stroke of midnight. They promised,' she says.

Anton's mum walks ahead of them into the luxuriously decorated home. The further in they go, the louder the voices and music become. Anton's mum turns down the volume.

'Look who we have here,' she shouts, pointing to Liv and Martina with both her arms.

Seven pairs of eyes turn towards them. They are all very clearly heavily intoxicated. Martina stares at Liv's dad in disgust.

'We just thought we'd say hi and wish you a Happy New Year,' she says, surprised at how normal she sounds, despite the sense of unease running amok in her body. Her mother totters towards them with two glasses of champagne and hands them over. She kisses them on the cheeks. She stinks of booze. Smoke. Lipstick. The faint odour of sweat. Martina is grateful when Liv cheerily engages her in small talk so she doesn't have to. The air in the big room is warm and stale.

Max's dad approaches, raises a glass and clinks it with her.

'You having a good time over at ours?'

'A really good time. The food was out of this world. We've mostly been playing Monopoly.'

'That's good.'

'And how's it going over here?'

'Well, you know. It's been good. Good food, some dancing.'

Martina pictures him lunging at a ten-year-old Max with his raised fist. The boy in the leather jacket who sat in front of her in the classroom and who she cared so much about, even back then.

She hates him.

At the same time, she hears her mother hissing in her ear.

'Straighten up. You're standing there like a sack of bloody spuds.'

Martina forces her features into a minimal smile.

She'd like to scream that they should all die. Line them up in a row and tell them why, each and every one. But she doesn't.

She makes small talk with Max's dad while her thoughts are a couple of storeys below her. Where Max and Anton, according to the plan, are silently pulling the quad bike out into the snow and connecting it to the stilts. She hopes that they'll be done soon. She angles her wrist so that she can see the time and notices that there are ten minutes to go until midnight.

She catches Liv's eye and nods discreetly towards the front door. She wants to get out of there. Away from these people and their lies and their darkness. Liv responds to the gesture with a wink.

'Right, it's time for us to leave you in peace,' Martina says, putting a hand on Max's dad's shoulder.

Martina keeps her eye on Liv to see whether she says goodbye to her parents, but Liv doesn't dignify them with so much as a look. She heads directly for the front door, straight-backed and head held high.

'I hate them so fucking much,' Martina whispers when they reach the hallway.

'Me too,' Liv replies, and Martina notices she has tears in her eyes.

'Have you had a change of heart?' she whispers.

'No, not at all,' Liv says hoarsely.

As the front door closes behind them, Martina puts her mobile to her ear.

'Are you ready?' she asks the boys, who are somewhere beneath the house.

She can only hear breathing and subdued footsteps.

'Hello?' she says.

'Sorry. This bloody quad bike is heavier than you'd think. Soon,' Max pants.

'What should Liv and I do?' Martina asks.

'Go back to my house. We'll sort out the rest. Stand by the window and enjoy.'

12

The garage smells of petrol and damp – scents that Anton has loved for as long as he can remember. The quad bike was a fifteenth birthday present and he got sick of it six months later. He pulls aside the olive-green tarpaulin. Max looks at the black vehicle with admiration.

'Do you remember when we drove into Stockholm on it?'

Anton laughs.

'For burgers, right?'

Max shakes his head.

'It was kebabs.'

Their parents are somewhere above their heads. In a house that soon won't exist. Anton begins to root through the boxes and cupboard for chains, but all he can find are spare lengths of rope from his father's boat.

'Do you think this will do?' he asks, holding up a couple of metres of rope.

Max comes over and puts his hands on the rope, tugging and pulling at it. He nods.

'Yeah, for sure.'

They pick two of the ropes, lay them out on the dirty cement floor and measure them in paces.

'Almost ten metres. That should do it.'

Anton takes the key for the quad bike from the cupboard, inserts it into the ignition and turns it – without starting the engine. Instead, he puts it into neutral and releases the brake.

Max puts the rope on the seat, braces himself and pushes from behind. Music is booming out, muffled by the closed windows. Europe, 'The Final Countdown'. On the other side of the water and in the other gardens, celebrations have already begun. Rockets are soaring into the sky, exploding. Anton glances at Max, who is grimacing with exertion. Sweat is glistening on his brow as he uses the muscles in his legs to move the machine forward. They've decided not to start the engine until the very last moment.

Max holds up the palm of his hand towards Anton. They stop. Exhale.

They're standing side by side under the terrace, inspecting the wooden stilts that hold up the house.

'Do you know which one is rotten?' Max asks.

'All of them, I think.'

They go up to one and gingerly illuminate the timber with Max's mobile phone. The wood looks brittle and porous. Anton runs a finger over it and grimaces when a splinter burrows into his skin.

'Let's go for the two closest ones.'

'At the same time?' Anton asks.

'If we can. Let's get the ropes – and take care they don't see you from the house. They're sure to head out onto the terrace at any moment to toast the New Year.'

Anton and Max creep back towards the quad bike, which they've positioned at an angle behind the house so as not to be seen. They each pick up a rope, carrying them in their arms towards the stilts. They knot them with firm, deft movements around two of the stilts. They stretch out the ropes and carry the other ends back to the quad bike. Attach them to the rear mounting. Anton catches sight of the strait and the water as a firework goes off with a bang – it's shiny, like oil.

Anton can see Max glancing at his phone and gestures quizzically towards him.

'One minute to go,' Max hisses.

At that moment, the terrace door opens. The music that has been enclosed by the windows pounds out over the water. The bass makes Anton's guts turn over.

'Perfect,' Max mouths at him.

Anton doesn't reply.

He clenches his fist, directing his gaze up to the terrace. He can make out the shadows. The laughter. The joy. He turns his head. Looks at Max's house. There, in the window, he thinks he can make out the contours of Liv's and Martina's bodies.

He waves and sees a rapid movement in reply.

He takes a deep breath.

Then he sits down and grips the handlebars.

'Twenty seconds to go,' Max hisses. 'Good luck.'

His friend ducks around the corner of the house and heads up towards the road to unlock the garage at his house, so that they can hide the quad bike there afterwards.

Anton begins to count down in his head, but he's too slow. He only makes it to fifteen before the sky explodes. Fireworks are going off on the street, in the gardens, along the water. The noise is deafening. It makes the ground and the big house shake.

There's no chance that anyone can hear the quad bike through that din. He turns the key and the vehicle springs to life. The engine roars but is drowned out by the cannonade of New Year celebrations. He switches into first gear, glances one final time at the house and gives it full throttle.

PART 4

13

Liv is standing at the window with Martina's arm around her shoulders. The boys are out there in the dark, moving quickly, hurrying about under the house, dragging ropes, talking. Eventually, only Anton is visible, straddling the quad bike. Liv didn't see when Max retreated. She peers out into the darkness. Anton is sitting there straight-backed. She can't see his face, but she can sense that it is grim and dogged.

When the sky explodes, Martina lets out a cry. Then she bends forward so that her brow is almost touching the glass.

'What's he waiting for?' she whispers anxiously to Liv.

Before Liv has time to reply, the quad bike suddenly lights up. A second later, it tears away. Liv closes her eyes.

At first nothing happens.

Then the stilts give way.

One by one, they snap like matchsticks.

First, the huge terrace collapses. Then the rest of the building. The house is dashed to pieces on the rocks and the ruins slide into the ice-cold water.

Martina screams loudly. Liv smiles.

A few minutes later, the boys tumble into the house. They rush over to the window and look out. Anton's house has collapsed. Only fragments remain. The people inside it are dead, or in the icy cold water, fighting for their lives.

But there's no help to be had.

When the police and paramedics arrive in the street, the four teenagers rush out to the scene. They play their roles well. Screaming. Crying. Tearing at their hair and shouting for their parents.

But inside, they're happy.

And free.

Acknowledgements

First and foremost, I'd like to thank my family. Without them, there would be no books. Simon, Wille, Meja, Charlie and Polly: you not only inspire me but also give me goals and create meaning to what I do.

It should also be said that books, despite what many people think, are the result of teamwork. And there are many people to thank. The whole gang at Forum, my publisher Ebba Östberg, and my freelance editor Olivia Demant. Everyone at Nordin Agency, especially my agent Joakim Hansson. I've really appreciated the help and support of Lili Assefa, my publicist and manager. I'd also like to thank my friend and uber talented collegue Pascal Engman, who has been a rock and a sounding board in the genesis of these books.

A WOMAN WHO HAS EVERYTHING...

People would kill to have Faye Adelheim's life.
She lives in a beautiful apartment, she has a gorgeous
husband who gives her everything she's ever wanted, and
she has an adorable daughter who lights up her world.

OR DOES SHE?

So how is it, then,
that Faye now finds herself in a police station?

THE TRUTH IS ABOUT TO COME OUT...

The truth is that Faye's life is far from what it seems. And
now she's been caught out. There's no way she's going
down without a fight. The only question is
– who will escape with their life?

ONE WOMAN...

Faye Adelheim seems to have it all. The head of a global business, she lives in a beautiful villa in Italy with her daughter. But in reality, her life is far from perfect.

ONE MAN...

Faye's ex-husband went to prison for murder. And now, he has escaped, with one thing on his mind. Revenge.

ONE FIGHT FOR SURVIVAL...

Faye will do anything to keep her family safe.
But this will be the toughest battle of her life.
And not everyone will live to tell the tale.

A SHOCKING MURDER...

It's a case unlike anything detective Mina Dabiri
has seen before. A woman trapped inside a magician's
box, with swords pierced through. But this time,
it's not a magic trick. It's murder.

A CASE WHICH TWISTS AND TURNS...

Knowing she has a terrifying killer on her hands, Mina enlists
the help of celebrity mentalist, Vincent Walder. Only he can give
her an insight into the secret world of magic and illusions.

A TICKING CLOCK TO STOP A SERIAL KILLER...

Mina and Vincent soon discover that the murder victim has the roman
numeral III engraved on her leg. The killer is counting down. There are
going to be three more murders. And time is running out to stop them.

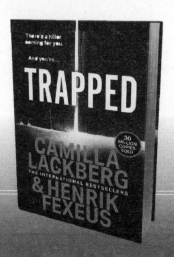